SON OF BLACK BEAUTY

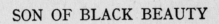

SON OF
BLACK BEAUTY

by

PHYLLIS BRIGGS

Abridged Edition

By arrangement with
THE THAMES PUBLISHING CO.
LONDON

PRINTED IN
DEAN &
41/43 Ludgate Hill

GREAT BRITAIN
SON Ltd.
LONDON E.C.4

TRADE MARK

MADE AND PRINTED IN GREAT BRITAIN BY PURNELL AND SONS, LTD.
PAULTON (SOMERSET) AND LONDON

603 03042 4

To
ADA WALLACE

PUBLISHER'S NOTE

In this book the art of the storyteller has been enlisted to produce what Black Beauty the horse could not—a son. This happy idea has enabled Phyllis Briggs to write a story in the same fine tradition as Anna Sewell's much-loved classic.

CONTENTS

CHAPTER ONE

SON OF BLACK BEAUTY

I AM now a very, very old horse, for I have lived to the great age of thirty years. But I am happy now and peaceful after a stormy life of adventures.

Many of my worries and hard times came upon me because I was wild and headstrong. I imagined that I could please myself all the time, which is good for nobody, men or horses. It is for this reason I want to tell all young colts starting out in life all about myself, so that they can keep out of some of the troubles I found.

I had better begin at the very beginning. Tradition has it that the great Black Beauty, whose goodness and patient temper have become famous, was my father. But if it is so, I did not inherit any of his gentle willingness to do my best.

I was born on a wild March night when great gales were banging in from the Channel, and the inky clouds were torn into ragged wisps which scurried across the sky. Of course, I do not remember anything about it, but I've heard old Gipsy Jacko tell about it so often that I can almost see it. My mother thought I was a long time getting on to my legs. She lay beside me looking at me, her long neck stretched out, her tired old eyes appearing almost hollow in the dancing shadows from the swinging lantern on old Jacko's caravan. Jacko was the leader of the little travelling band who owned my mother and me. At last she butted me gently with her head. "Don't be idle, son," she said quietly. "It's one of the worst ways to begin life. A colt should be able to keep up with his mother at a gallop within a few hours of birth!"

Hearing this, I tried very hard to get up. My fuzzy head felt silly and top-heavy, and my legs were wobbly and no good at all. But I managed to kneel up and look about me, and I must say my first glimpse of life was rather scaring.

There were two big caravans and a cart, but from the doors and windows streamed out nice comforting light, and they looked gay and cosy. Old Gipsy Jacko's wife, Brown Joan, was pottering in and out of the first caravan, putting the youngsters to bed. Every time her head and shoulders came between the lantern and us, they made a big woolly shadow that stretched out over the meadow like a giant hand groping to catch something.

I should have been pretty scared if it had not been for my mother, who lay patiently there, nosing at the grass in a weary way as if she was too spent to eat. She looked at me again as I struggled to get up.

"That's right, son. Do everything with a will and spirit, and you will get on even if I am not there to help you."

At that, I made another terrific effort and got up, to stand swaying in that heady wind. A man came out of the shadows, and he was big and rough, but not with the roughness that is horrid. His old jacket and trousers were rough, teazled into a kind of fur from much contact with blackthorn hedges and the hard going of a gipsy's life. His dear old face and head were rough with hair, for Gipsy Jacko never shaved or used a brush in all his life. But his old eyes were as kind as the blue periwinkle flowers shining in a copse-tangle, and his hands were as gentle as any I have ever known.

"Joan, come quickly! Bring me a pail of hot water," he shouted, with a kind of strained urgency. "The mare's in a bad way. Andrea, lad, come here and take charge of the foal. Look lively, lad!"

Then I saw Andrea, and I took to him at once. He had not been sent to bed with the children, for he was older than they, though still a mancolt, as men count age. Someone said he was fifteen. He was like a larch-pole for straightness, and his eyes were black as the shadows cast on a summer night at full-moon. He came over to me, and I didn't feel I wanted to jump away. I put my head forward towards him, and he put his hand on my neck and talked slowly in soothing tones.

"Come along, little fellow, come along with me. We must find you something in place of the milk you have a right to expect. Come, come along."

I didn't hang back, but wobbled after him round to the other side of the caravan, where there were the remains of one of last year's haystacks—cut down, it is true, but still a pleasant shelter. Three horses were picketed there and the ground was springy with tumbled hay.

Andrea made me lie down and then he went off and filled a bottle with milk, which he brought me. How delicious it tasted, and how eagerly I sucked it down while he held the bottle and tilted it, stroking me and talking all the time till I felt friendly and somewhat comforted.

"I like you," he whispered to me. "Perhaps old Jacko will give you to me so you can be my horse and I will train you. What fun you and I could have!"

I could not answer him, and at the time I don't suppose I understood what he was talking about, but I looked eagerly after the bottle of milk when it was all gone. Andrea was very good, for he sat by me all that night, so that I did not miss my mother, and in the morning I could not find her. I never saw her again.

If she had lived she could have given me so much advice

which would have helped me to avoid some of my later mistakes. As it was, I was left all alone in the world. If it had not been for Andrea I should have felt miserable. But I soon got to look for him, and the very sound of his cheery young voice made my heart feel good and warm.

The gipsies broke camp the next morning. The last thing that I remember of that first camping-ground of my wandering life was the sight of one of the young children laying a little bunch of heavy-headed dandelions on a low mound where the earth had been newly dug. The cheery gold of those early blooms shone in the grey light of dawn like a little banner of hope.

Andrea had lifted me into the cart on to a piece of nice sacking, and there I lay, craning up my neck in great curiosity to see over the low side at the truly wonderful world. The March gale had not blown itself out yet, but the sky was quite clear of cloud and was a real spring blue. The edges of the road were starred with celandines, and a smell of sap rose from the red buds of the young birches as their thin branchlets tossed and thrashed.

Andrea climbed in beside me and took up the reins, for the cart was in his charge. I must say I was glad to have him so near me, for I knew there was something I missed and wanted, but I could not say what it was or why there was something frightening and lonely about that morning.

During the next few months I grew quickly and thrived, for Andrea never let me go very long without a kind word or look. I was happy as the larks that shrilled their songs over the red ploughlands of that lovely southern county on the Channel coast. Sometimes, I felt so happy and full of bubbling fun that I frolicked and kicked for the sheer love of it, and Andrea would laugh and clap his hands. Old Jacko would look at me, and rub his bristly chin till I thought he would prick himself.

One day, he said: "Andrea, lad, there's blood and breeding in that colt. He's no farm-horse. Look at his eye and the long clean limbs of him! Yes, you shall have him for your own. But break and train him carefully—he may be difficult. Bottle-fed youngsters are not always easy to deal with, and he's more nervous than I quite like. What are you going to call him?"

"I don't know. I can't think of a name that really fits him," the boy said, and he stroked my shoulder as I nibbled the sweet grass and tossed my fine tail, which was becoming long and silky.

"Jet-black, he is," the boy went on musingly. "No, not quite black. There's that star on his face and some white hair above the star as if it had been smudged a wee bit!"

"That's the stardust." The old man laughed at the boy's fancies.

"That's it! That's a wonderful name for him—Stardust," the boy cried. "Just like the trail of light a meteor leaves behind it as it flies so fast on November nights. And that's what he is going to do, I know. He's going to gallop and fly like a meteor, and he is the colour of the night. Stardust, it shall be; Stardust, son of Black Beauty!"

CHAPTER TWO

GIPSY JACKO

THE GIPSIES were making their way slowly westward all that spring and summer, and wherever they went I, of course, went too. We would camp sometimes for days and weeks in one place, till it felt almost like home and I got to know every field and copse and path.

Brown Joan was one of the busiest women I ever saw, for she did all the work of those travelling homes, and kept the caravans as bright and clean as could be. The spotted curtains at the tiny windows were often out bleaching on the hedges, and she was as often washing the children as their little clothes.

But she found time even then to weave rush mats, make pegs, and flowers from wood-shavings, and gather berries and wild fruit and flowers to sell from door to door. Sometimes, at the word "gipsies" the village women would shut their doors, but one look at Brown Joan's face made them waver. She was exactly like one of those apples, wind-blown into the long grass, to lie unnoticed, wrinkling and fading till it looked like a brown-leather ball creased into smiles. Her eyes were as merry as a robin's, and no thing of fur or feather ever fled from her.

I loved to have her pat my coat, and she often groomed me, for she was as strong as a man. With the curry-comb strapped to the back of one hand, and the brush in the other, she would work at my coat till it shone, and she sang gipsy songs to me all the time. Horses love being talked and sung to. I don't think the other horses got nearly the attention that I did, and I began to think of myself as a little bit better than they were. One, called Jock, was a nice little cobby-horse with a happy disposition and a willingness to work that I sometimes thought a trifle stupid. The other two were an old white horse called Bob, and Sandy, a bay.

I was growing into a very fine fellow indeed and I was so full of life that I think sometimes old Gipsy Jacko would watch me dubiously. I was with these good people for about five years, so I may as well tell you something about him, too. He owned the bigger of the two caravans, and his younger brother had the other, which was always drawn by Jock. I had little to do with him as it was old Jacko who owned me and the other horses. Jacko often took a temporary job at farms we passed in the busy season, and often Andrea would go with him. At thatching time he could twist the wonderful patterns from the gleaming wheat-straw till they looked like elaborate carvings in golden wood. He could doctor cattle and sick sheep, and on lambing nights they used to say: "No need to have a vet for they difficult ewes. Old Jacko's sitting along of they, and the lantern's down at his feet so's the light will not vex the poor creatures."

I believe that often the little lambs would be as happy letting him hold them wrapped in his fuzzy old coat as they would be snuggling up to their woolly mothers. He could tell just when a hive was going to swarm, and he could take it and house it in its new hive with no gloves or veil to guard him, and yet he used to say no bee had ever stung him in his life.

A gentleman-farmer at whose place we had called for permission to camp in his big field had sufficient interest to come and inspect us. He took a great liking to Jacko and asked him why he didn't quit the wandering life and settle to something permanently useful.

"I'd find you work on my place all the year," he said.

But Jacko shook his head. "It's no manner of use, sir, for me or my wife either. We'd be broken things if we couldn't up sticks and off when the fancy took us. There is no music like the summer song of the wind in the larches or the prattle of tumbling water on a stony stream-bed."

The man tried hard to persuade Gipsy Jacko, and when he saw me the wonder in his face grew.

"That young horse of yours has the build of a racer, gipsy. He is as out of place here in your camp as I am!"

Jacko patted me as he answered, smiling: "I hope he is not doomed to draw gipsy vans all his life. I think he will rise in the world. I have given him to my son and when he has broken and trained him he will probably sell him well."

I was very excited when I heard this and from that moment I began secretly to despise the gipsies wandering contentedly over the wolds and commons with their few poor possessions. I quite agreed with the farmer; I was destined for better things! I wondered when Andrea would begin to train me.

Of course, I was quite used to being led about with an old rope-halter, but I realised there was more to come. My breaking-in came when I was quite grown-up. Andrea taught me to wear a bit, and with great patience made me understand what I was to do when he guided me and led me about. The bit, pressing down on my tongue, irritated me, and I pranced and kicked, I fear only half playfully. But he never struck me or punished me; he only went on with great patience. He spent many days and weeks over my training and each day I felt a finer horse, and wondered what sort of a home I should go to when I was sold.

But the days passed and the seasons came and went. The months of blossom and the months of harvest came round, the corn-cockles and the poppies passed away, the winter frosts blackened the world.

Pictures of those days come back to me as strongly as visions in a camp-fire. I remember the day when I was taken for my first pairs of shoes. I was afraid of the hot interior of the farrier's shed and the flashes of white-hot light from the forge-fire. The noise of the hammering frightened me too, and if it had not been that Andrea was with me, I should have fretted and kicked and won free before they could do to me the dreadful things I feared.

When I found that I was expected always to wear those queer, heavy, steel shoes, and that each month they must be inspected and removed and perhaps be replaced by new ones I felt angry and terrified.

"Take care, lad," the smith cried. "He's laid his ears back and shown the whites of his eyes. That horse has no business to be in your camp. He is made for speed and glory!"

Andrea came up to me and, fearlessly as ever, stood close to my shoulder with his arm flung over me. He leaned his head against me and I stopped trembling and sweating.

"Stardust shall have his chance," he said moodily. "But I don't want the day to come. Get on with your work, smith. We haven't got all the night to chatter."

I felt proud and pleased that Andrea was my master when I saw the respectful way the man obeyed him. There was something about the common gipsy lad which made people give way to him and obey him. I found too that the gipsies in our little camp usually shoed the horses themselves but that the boy had determined that I should have the very best of everything. I realised how much I loved and looked up to him.

I remember well the first really hard ride I had, and it was for Andrea's sake.

CHAPTER THREE

FARMER DOWLING'S BEES

IT WAS one very hot summer day. Andrea often rode me and we would go the rounds of the outlying farms together, selling the things that Brown Joan had made.

I felt a bit sulky about the big rough basket I was expected to carry on my glossy back in front of Andrea, but I enjoyed those rides, and always capered and pranced to show how pleased I was.

"Gently, boy; steady down," Andrea would say, and each time old Jacko would shake his head.

"All very well with us who love him," he muttered. "But with his spirit, if ever he comes up against life, it may go ill with his temper."

On this day, just as we were starting, Gipsy Jacko came out of the big caravan. "Stop at Farmer Dowling's and get a little honey," he said.

So, that day, we took Farmer Dowling's wide acres into our road and trotted up to the old red-brick farmhouse. White pigeons were lazily cooing, nodding their heads in time to their own music. Gnats danced and wavered, and the farm dog, too hot to bark, shuffled and clanked his chain as if to show he was alert and no one had better start any nonsense. Beyond the house under the orchard-trees were the hives, the air above them alive with a cloud of bees.

A short, fat woman was moving along by the fence. She walked lame; in fact could only hobble. She turned at the sound of hooves and her face was lined with worry.

"Oh, thank goodness!" she cried at sight of us. "It's young Andrea, isn't it? The old man's away to town, and, of course, on this day of all two of the hives must swarm. Both of them are in the linden yonder, and I know naught of bees—they're his hobby. I'm thankful they're low down on the boughs, and maybe if old Jacko would spare the time to come and take them for me——"

"I'm right sure he will!" Andrea dismounted, while I stood snorting and flicking my tail against the flies, twitching my skin to keep them from settling. The boy could not resist just going up to the fence to see the bees, which were hanging in the tree. They looked like a bag of glistening moving black beads; something about that crawling mass and the deep hum from the hives terrified me so that I began to sweat and tremble, as I always did when afraid. I hung back, but I could not escape, as the reins were looped over the boy's arm.

Perhaps our appearance or the thud of our footfalls alarmed the insects; I don't know how it was, but all at once the swarm rose in the air still in its compact form and, like a dark cloud, drove across to us. I gave a scream of fear and reared, but it was Andrea who was unlucky. The swarm settled on his neck and shoulders just as if he were wearing a black cape. It was a mercy they kept off his face.

As it was, it was the most terrible thing that could well happen to anyone. One second of panic, one frantic effort to sweep away the clinging mass, and the boy would be stung to death. His face, despite its tan, went white as the lime they spread upon the fields in spring. I heard him tell Gipsy Jacko long afterwards that it took all the grit and red courage he possessed to stand there motionless.

"Mercy on us!" the woman screamed. "What'll I do— what will I *do*?"

"Can you find the queen?" the boy muttered thickly.

"Take her off and put her in an empty hive. They'll follow. But be quick! I can't stand this much longer."

"I don't know one bee from another," the woman wailed helplessly. "Oh, what'll I do?"

"Then get on the horse and fetch Jacko, and make haste."

I stood by in a ferment of fear, but I realised suddenly how much Andrea meant to me. I was no longer afraid of the bees for myself, but trembled for my young master. With feeble little moans of distress, Mrs. Dowling hobbled to me and caught up the slack reins which Andrea had let fall. I had never had anyone but the boy on my back, and for one instant I thought of running away from this halting strange woman in the flapping grey skirts, which were so long that to ride at all she must roll her petticoats to her knees.

But in emergencies who cares for anything? I loved Andrea and he was in trouble and I must get this fat, heavy thing to our camp so that Jacko could come and save him. So I stood as still as the boy while Mrs. Dowling climbed on the fence for a mounting-block and somehow managed to flop across my back.

"Get up," she urged. "Where is the camp, boy?"

"By the valley meadow!"

I needed no urging, I can tell you. I understood what was wanted and all I hoped was that the farmer's wife could hold on. I cleared the first gate, for there was no time to stop, dismount and get it open. Mrs. Dowling just gave a kind of strangled cry of horror and flung her arms around my neck, burying her red face in my black mane.

She had never been a horsewoman, having been thrown when only a girl. She had lost her nerve after that, so that it speaks much for her that that day she did what she did. As for me, I was so keyed up with the idea of fetching help that nothing seemed too hard.

I believe I could have cleared the tree-tops as I felt then. Down the sandy road I galloped, and it was well I knew the way and where I was going, for Mrs. Dowling never spoke a word of guidance to me, but only clung in desperation till I felt I was being throttled.

Never in all my life did the painted caravans look so pleasant and reassuring, and when old Jacko, fortunately still in camp, came from the back where he had been peeling potatoes over a tin pail, I could have reared and kicked from sheer delight and relief.

"Hey, what's this, what's all this?" Jacko shouted in great alarm at sight of us. He helped the farmer's wife down and listened to her breathless explanation, while the children clung about us and Brown Joan came forward anxiously.

Old Jacko waited only till he had the facts clearly and then he vaulted on my back and drove his heels against my sides.

"Up, lad, off we go," he cried and I was as eager as he to start to the rescue. As we flashed down the meadow I had a last glimpse of Mrs. Dowling being helped by Brown Joan into the caravan to take a dish of tea to restore her tranquillity.

We had not taken very long to do the two miles from the farm to the camp, but we beat all records going back. Old Jacko could ride and he helped me so much that in only a very short time we were back at the farm, where the boy still stood half crouching, his hands gripping the top rail of the fence convulsively.

In two minutes the old gipsy had taken the swarm and the boy was free. The other swarm in the linden had lifted and gone—none knew where.

"Don't thank me; it's Stardust deserves the credit," Jacko said. "He had the storm-wind in his heels, lad. He ought to run on the heath at Newmarket with those legs. Speed—talk of whirlwinds rather."

The boy hugged me and patted me and I had a queer feeling of warmth round my heart. He said very little, but *I* knew how much he loved me, and I was happy and content just to have him by me again.

CHAPTER FOUR

THE STRANGE NEW FOOD

Two DAYS later there came a present from the farmer for me, and Andrea opened the sack himself. It was full of the very best oats, more than he had ever seen before. Oats were expensive and we horses did not expect them very often; certainly I had never had so much at once. Unknown to Jacko, Andrea gave me an over-generous feed, and I relished it greatly.

It was the most wonderful food I had ever tasted and I began to wish I could have it often—at every meal perhaps. The old white horse, Bob, was tethered near me and he had also been given some oats, but the boy had not been so heavy-handed with his helping. As he munched his portion he shook his head and fly-twitched his skin.

"Oats do funny things to some horses," he said. "I'm surprised they gave you so much when you're not used to it."

"How do you mean—funny?" I asked rather crossly, for it nettled me to hear this common old white horse criticise my young master.

"Well, it makes them skittish," he snorted into his food-pail, blowing out little wisps of chaff. "And seeing you are skittish most of the time I should think it could be dangerous!"

The other two horses said nothing, but finished their food in silence. Of course, I have in after years discovered that the white horse was quite right in what he said. A horse I once knew could not take a single oat, and they had to be kept right out of his diet or else he would kick over the traces, his legs would swell, and he would set out in a pretty general way to wreck everything in sight.

But at the time I was only angry and would not reply, so the old white horse finished his feed in philosophic silence and then stood dreaming, head drooped low in peaceful content, tail switching idly.

Soon I began to feel restive and could not keep my feet still. I began to prance and sidle, and I longed to be free so that I could gallop madly away and escape, where and from what I did not know and did not care so long as I could race out into the world, flying at top speed over fence and field and ditch.

I'm not sure that I wanted Andrea with me. Freedom and headlong racing—it was in my blood. I wanted to hear my steel shoes drumming on the road, I wanted to scatter the shingle with my flying hooves, I wanted never again to stop. If only horses could have wings like birds, I must have thought, so that I need not stay on the ground but gallop and soar for ever!

Brown Joan was coming back from a round selling brushes, and she took one startled look at me and then called the boy.

"Andrea, come here! You'll have to take the black horse for a turn of exercise or there'll be trouble," she cried. "He's got fireworks in his feet for sure!"

Men should be more careful of the poor dumb beasts in their charge. *We* can't speak and ask for the things we need, sometimes things which are vital for our comfort or health. Real animal-lovers are always on the alert and know almost as soon as we do what we lack, but the heedless, careless, indolent humans who look upon us as some kind of intelligent machine—they are to be feared and shunned. I was very lucky in my master, and in Gipsy Jacko and Brown Joan.

Andrea came running and when he saw me he untethered me quickly, slipped on a bridle and without waiting for more leaped up to ride me bareback, as he often did. Not that he meant to do more than give me some gentle exercise; he was too clever with horses to make the mistake of giving them heavy exercise too soon after feeding.

But I had other ideas! As soon as he was up, my blood seemed to boil over. I was absolutely fizzing with suppressed energy. I reared high on my hind legs, pawing at the air. I must have been a fine sight, I dare say. My long, silky, jet-black mane and tail streamed out in the wind, my eyes were flashing with excitement, and the sunshine glittered on my shoes. Andrea must have looked equally well. His skin was burned to an Indian darkness and his teeth were like chips of ivory when he smiled. Only he was not smiling now. Blue, tattered trousers, cut off at the knee, and an open shirt were all the clothes he wore. He was bare-headed and his hair curled like a black water-dog's. He held on by the sheer muscular strength of his knees.

Up and up I reared, staggering backwards on my hind legs till I began to wonder if I should fall crashing, and I was in such a queer mood that I really did not altogether care. A fleeting wish passed through my mind that as I was beginning to be frightened at myself the boy could do something to stop me, for I did not seem to be able to help myself.

Then I felt Andrea lean forward so that his face was almost hidden by my flying mane.

"Talk of meteors!" he gasped. "Come off it, Stardust!"

A lean, muscular hand shot out and gripped my windpipe; fingers as strong as a carpenter's vice closed on it, cutting off my breath. It was a clever horseman's trick to bring down a rearing horse and I knew at once that he was master of me, and to tell the truth I was glad it was so.

As soon as I had dropped back to earth again he released me and I sucked down lungfuls of sweet air, and shook myself, snorting and trembling.

"Come on, old boy," Andrea said; "we'll go for a nice little round and end up later with a stretching gallop. Cheerily does it!"

He was patting me and talking to me, and so, with a final springy caper, I started off. Brown Joan stood watching us out of sight, her curved old hand hooding her eyes against the sun. Their fingers at their mouths in vague fear, the younger children huddled about her, their fists clutching her fruit-stained old apron.

Andrea turned me up on to the high road and I felt at once much more easy. The prickle and ache were going out of my feet and I was calming down and steadying. He knew it was not vice but only youthful high spirits brought on by over-feeding. He knew too that I was unusually nervy and excitable, for no foal brought up by hand faces life with quite the same qualities as one who has been fed and taught by a careful, patient mother.

All would have gone well this time if it had not been for an unfortunate thing that no one could have foreseen. Some children were trailing home from school, their satchels on their backs, their fingers black with the juice from bunches of dandelions they were industriously picking. One round-cheeked boy with mischievous eyes had a stout paper bag in his hands and he was inflating it with a thoroughness of effort which he probably did not bring to his lessons. When it was well blown out, taut and swelling, he held it tightly closed in his left hand, waiting to burst it with his right, while he looked round in impish fun to see if there was anyone near that he could scare.

Of course, at the time, I did not know what he was going to do and had never even seen a paper bag. But even today

I cannot see one without feeling again a tremor of sick fear as memory comes flooding back.

The boy caught sight of us, and, waiting till we were almost abreast, he burst his paper bag. I think that Andrea was nearly as startled as I was. Hot fear rushed over me and in maddened terror I was off and away. I knew the boy was shouting to me, striving to keep his voice natural so as not to alarm me any more. He tried to check me, but he might have been a feather on my back for all the good his efforts did. For the first and last time in my life I took the bit between my teeth and bolted, completely out of control.

A sharp bend in the road ahead I disdained, and, instead of taking it, I gathered myself to clear the hawthorn hedge to the right. Andrea knew by instinct what I was going to do, and, clever lad that he was, instead of trying to stop me, which might have brought us both down in ruin, he leaned forward and helped me all he could. I think I must have had a good two feet of clearance as I sailed over like a summer butterfly.

The drop into the field on the inside was steeper than I had thought, but in my panic flight it would have taken more than that to stop me. We fled across that field swifter than the shadows of the storm-clouds darken the grass. A wide stream was cleared with many feet to spare. On my back the boy still clung, waiting any chance to help me, watchful as an eagle. I knew how his cheeks would be flaming with excitement, his black eyes snapping.

I nearly came down in the next field when an old cock-pheasant sprang with a great clattering of pinions almost from under my thundering feet. But I recovered myself and galloped on. Ahead was a low embankment and fence, and in the distance was a growing rumble of sound descending towards us from the direction of a big market-town five miles away.

"Stop, stop!" Andrea was beginning to urge me, and his voice had a certain cold quality in it which betrays the man who is suddenly afraid and is trying to put a force on himself to hide it. "Stardust! The express is coming! That's the main-line ahead. Stop it. Whoa, I say!"

Foam was flying backwards from my working mouth, foam flecked with blood, for I had hurt my tongue when I clamped down hard on the bit. My lovely black coat was darker still with sweat, but I raced up that embankment as if it had been level, and, collecting every ounce of energy, took the difficult upward jump over the fence at the top.

The effort took something out of me and for the first time I began to flag. Before me were the flashing tracks of the railway, a thing I had never even imagined, and almost upon us was the black weight of the express, a ribbon of steam flying backwards, the wheels screaming with speed.

"We're lost!" The exclamation was almost a sob from the boy upon my back. Something new awoke in my heart, love for something beside myself and my own will. In that shattering moment I felt I must save him, cost me what it might. It was too late to slack; my feet were upon the metals; so I strained my last muscle in a frantic dash across under the very lamps of the express.

We were over, and I had slipped and galloped stumblingly down a straight bank on the other side and plunged head-long into a lake of water, where at last I managed to stop. I stood shivering there, the muddied water weaving past my trembling legs, my head drooping. Andrea, who had been tossed over my head as lightly as a ball is thrown, rose dripping and stumbled to his feet. He came to my side, and with cold, shaking hands felt me over anxiously, while the express tore shrieking into the distance.

"Stardust, boy," he whispered, "it was all my fault. But

only you could have galloped like that and only you could have saved us. But it worries me to think what might happen if you were with anyone who did not understand— out in the world—where men are so hard on each other and on their four-footed friends."

CHAPTER FIVE

THE SHINY-FACED MAN

WE GOT home by easy stages that day. When you have nearly lost something that you love very much, and get it back safely, you are quite content to go on quietly just for the time being, happy in the knowledge that, after all, the worst has not happened.

I was very tired and my head felt heavy. Andrea did not ride, but walked at my side, and I kept nudging him and lipping at his hands to try and show him what I felt.

"That's all right, Stardust," he told me over and over again as he patted my neck.

At the camp they were amazed to see us return with no bones broken. Gipsy Jacko felt me all over, muttering and shaking his head. But he rubbed me down and made me very comfortable. I think he was rather sharp with Andrea, for he could not bear carelessness towards dumb animals, in any form, and he would not believe that his own son could have been so stupid.

They both came to me again later, and Andrea was a bit tight-lipped and white under his tan, but he flung his arms round my neck and stood silently by, his face hidden in my mane.

"Don't fret," the old man advised quietly. "You haven't lost him. With brains like his he'd have got you out of worse jams than that. You could teach that horse nearly anything! He is one of the rare ones who can *think*!"

Perhaps it was these words which gave Andrea the idea, but after that he began teaching me tricks. At first I could not make out what he was at, but soon it became a great game with us and I enjoyed it nearly as much as he did. We horses know simple numbers, of course, but we can't count in our heads like men can. But in show-business there are quite a number of tricks which make it look as if we can, and it amazes and amuses people. I can't quite remember how he first got the idea across to me, but he stood with one hand on my withers, where the slightest pressure of his fingers could be felt. Each time he pressed he taught me to paw at the ground once, and this I could do very well, for I had a great habit of pawing the ground, anyway.

I must have looked tremendously clever to anyone watching us. Gipsy Jacko would pretend to ask me. "What are four and five?" Andrea would give me the signals and I would paw the ground the correct number of times. Then they would both applaud in great glee, and I would toss my fine mane and snort and roll my eyes.

Then Andrea went on to teach me to watch for a signal even when he was not touching me; this was far more difficult but much more showy. He would stand in front of me with his arms folded across his broad chest and I would watch those brown hands anxiously, wishful to please him, though I did not understand what the use of the trick was, anyway.

Soon I could detect the smallest motion of one finger as he raised and lowered it, unnoticed by anyone standing near, for they were watching *me* to see if I would foozle the trick.

"That'll shake 'em all," Gipsy Jacko chuckled in huge delight. "There's a nice little extra source of income for you, Andrea, at fairs and shows. You'll be marrying and buying your own caravan soon."

But none of us could foresee where the thing was to take us.

I was nearly five years old when my life changed suddenly
and I said goodbye for the time to the open life I loved. It
was January, and the weather was quite bitter. The caravans
were parked on an empty lot in a big town in the Midlands
and the gipsies found a little more shelter from the bleakness
of the frost for themselves and their animals. Brown Joan
went selling from door to door, and the men found temporary
jobs. Andrea was quite a man now and he and I attracted
so much attention that often Jacko was worried, but he said
nothing. His son was six feet tall, broad-shouldered, and
handsome as a picture. When he laughed his teeth flashed
white in his brown face. He tied a red handkerchief round
his black locks, and wherever he went people turned and
stared after him. They stared after me too and I know
that Gipsy Jacko was afraid I should get stolen. People who
knew about horses said I was exactly like the painting of the
Godolphin Arabian, one of the most famous horses in history
and from whom many of the finest racers are descended.

The gipsies showed me off as little as possible and kept
very quiet about me so that I should not get stolen. It was
then, by the merest chance, that one day I saw the circus
come to town. The other horses were at work and there was
an errand to be done, so little Dan, as they called Andrea's
brother, said he would ride me. We were good friends and
he was now a big fellow of fifteen, thoughtful and hardworking. I could see that Gipsy Jacko and Brown Joan
were nervous about it, but they let us go.

I was overjoyed at the idea of the fun and exercise, and
tried not to be too eager, but I could not help being a bit
restive. The sparkling air was snapping with frost and it
made my blood tingle. I rather fear that little Dan had a
jolting time of it, but being a gipsy he stuck on and was not
afraid, so that presently I settled down and we had a grand
ride out into the country to do our errand.

I can still remember the look of the frost-hardened plough-lands with the rooks beating slowly by above them, the withered brown of the forgotten hedgerows where the children had gathered ragged robin and sheeps'-bit-scabious in the long-past summer days. They, the children, would not come again till another July, for they were all shut up in the dark schoolhouse in the town learning their criss-cross-row.

There were fingers of dagger-like ice on the brown of little streams and the earth rang hollowly below my hoofs. As we neared town on our return we saw the half-mile-long procession of the circus coming down the main road on its way in. I pricked my ears with interest.

"At least twenty big cars!" Dan cried aloud in his excitement. "All red and gold and blue, and, oh, those last ones have the wild beasts in them! Oh, oh!"

Packed into those painted cars was all the glitter and romance I was to come to know so well. We had halted in our little by-road to see them go by, and the boy slipped down and came to my head, where he stood panting with eager interest. He was nearly as excited as I was at the queerness of it all.

Slowly they rumbled towards us and drew abreast, and then I realised how big and heavy those cars were. Two big, powerful horses drew each one, and they made our caravans look like painted toys. After the first half-dozen came a troop of about fifty horses in the care of a dozen men. *Such* horses—with the arched necks, clean, strong limbs, wide nostrils and big gentle eyes which betrayed the Arab strain. There were sets of bays and blacks and chestnuts. They kicked up the frozen road-dust as they passed, so that the Shetland ponies following them were almost lost in the ring-ing clouds. Faded golden leaves from the hedges cart-wheeled in the draught of their passing.

I could not help it—I neighed a greeting to them and received an instant reply. Little Dan jumped for joy at my side. The men waved to us and shouted something, and they looked at me with great curiosity. Then came more cars, and then six which were all banded and barred with steel, and from them came a peculiar smell which made the hairs of my mane crest a trifle and my breath to shorten with fear. A musty, mousy smell, heavy with a threat of the unknown.

"The beasts, the lions and tigers!" Dan whispered to himself. "Oh, I can't wait to tell Andrea about this; he will be crazy with the thrill of it!"

Then came the biggest car of all, in which the owner of the circus travelled with his family and some of the leaders of the troupe. Four horses drew this car, and it rumbled and jarred its way past us. Sitting on the box, driving the four horses as unconcernedly as if there had been one only, was the most extraordinary man I ever saw. He was as short and broad as a barn-door, and in his loud check suit with patterns as big as bricks he appeared huge. His face was as round and red as a rising sun, but it was his eyes which held and fascinated all who met him. They were very small, hard and brown as glass buttons, and they did not miss a thing. You would think he was just looking about him casually as he stood switching at his big boots with the little cane he always carried, but afterwards he would talk about every last little thing in detail of what he had been gazing at.

Those strange hard eyes rested on us in our little lane, and their expression changed oddly, though not a muscle in his shiny red face so much as twitched. He raised a foghorn of a voice.

"Hey, boy, mount and ride along of my car a piece. I'd like a word with ye."

Overjoyed at this notice of us, Dan scrambled on my back, and guided me, sidling and a bit nervous, to ride, high-stepping and doubtful, in the dusty clouds by the car-wheels.

"That's a nice horse you're riding. Belong to your Dad, boy."

"No, to my brother," Dan said shyly.

"Think he'd care to sell?" asked the man, drawing the whip from its socket and cracking it suddenly so that I jumped. "Hmm, plenty of spirit! Splendid action!"

"I don't know." Dan hesitated, in a great quandary. "He used to say, sir, that he'd sell Stradust, but now I'm not so sure!"

"Well, you ask him," the shiny-faced man said easily. "If he's a personable young man I might find him a riding act."

Little Dan's face lighted up. "There's tricks, sir; he's taught Stardust some wonderful tricks."

Again the expression in those hard, but not unkind little eyes changed subtly. "Well, tell him to come along and see me. Who is he to ask for, you say? The owner, Melville's Circus. Now, boy, I won't keep you any longer. Ride on!"

CHAPTER SIX

THE CIRCUS

I was in a great state of excitement at all this. My ideas
had changed in the last year, so that now I did not want to
leave Andrea even if it meant getting out in the world and
bettering myself. But if we could go together—ah, that was
another bale of straw!

Talk buzzed in the gipsy camp on the windy allotment
that night. I was so impatient and worked up that I could
not eat any of my evening rations of hay. Animals are
sensitive to atmosphere. Men do not realise this, and wonder
that their own feelings and fears affect their mounts, making
them nervous and restive, too.

But at last Andrea came to me, as he always did last thing
to see I had all I wanted. They had an old shed on the
allotment which gave us quite a nice shelter these bitter
nights. I can still see the joy on my young master's face, the
shifting glow from the lantern reflecting redly on old Bob's
white coat, the stupid, patient faces of the other horses,
and a drift of dust from the kicked-up straw winking in the
light.

I knew from Andrea's expression and the way he patted
me that it was all settled. Next day he rode me to a field
where the circus had pitched camp; hard by was a big
wooden building, circular in shape, where many a passing
circus gave performances in winter when it was not to be
expected that the people would care to sit in a tent.

A row of the beautiful Arab liberty-horses were outside
being groomed, and they pricked their sensitive ears and one

whinnied to me in a very friendly way. There hung over everything the delicious smell of the sawdust ring, the scent of grease-paint and tinsel clothes, which have a smell all their own. The faces of the men grooming the horses and working about showed that they had grown up under many different skies. There were Spanish tumblers, Chinese acrobats and Indian jugglers. But white, chocolate or yellow-skinned, they were all busy helping with the every-day jobs, their show-tricks forgotten for the moment.

I pranced with delight and arched my fine neck. This seemed to me a very good place that I had come to. I *was* rising in the world. Why, at this rate, I might end in the Queen's stables!

"What do you want, boy?" a man asked Andrea, though the word "boy" hardly applied to the good-looking man who rode me with such skill and ease.

"I want to see the owner."

"Yes, that's right," said the shiny-faced man, coming forward from where he had been tightening a row of tent-pegs. "Come into the ring; your little brother said some-thing about performances. Let's see, let's see!"

He held my bridle and led us into the circular building where the ring was. All was echoing gloom and that dusty expectancy always felt in a place where things happen only by lamplight.

Melville lit a couple of oil-lamps, and their pools of yellow light made brilliant patches hemmed by the dark. I could see that the small brown eyes had taken in every detail of Andrea's figure and that the man was pleased. He was still more pleased when he saw the tricks which Andrea and I had practised many a time together.

"Capital!" he nodded, and straightway fell to discussing what wages he would pay. I think they must have been pretty good, for Andrea patted me and his eyes were happy and full of sparkling light, as they always were when he was pleased.

"Then that's settled," said the man. "I'll get your name on to the bills. Have today to settle in and you shall give your first performance tomorrow night. Let me see—we'll bill you as Gipsy Andrea and the famous Counting Horse from Arabia!"

"But," my young master objected, "he isn't from Arabia and he isn't famous!"

"He soon will be." Melville waved aside all such honest scruples. "You must appeal to the public, boy, or where are you? Why, sitting out in a rainy ditch without even a loaf of dry bread!"

I can't tell you how exciting that day was; first, I was led to some nice airy tents where the wonderful horses that I had admired were picketed in rows. By each horse stood two bright, clean pails, one for food and the other full of fresh water. There was plenty of dry, warm litter.

I was attracted instantly by a beautiful black horse standing next to me. Andrea had been taken to see his quarters, so I felt quite on my own. The black horse turned and looked at me.

"You're extremely like me," I suggested almost timidly, for, for the first time in my life, I felt strange and at a disadvantage.

"No, that I'm certainly not," the black horse answered somewhat sharply. "I've no star like you have. I am all black, which is a great deal finer, I consider. My name is Bluegrass and I come from America. My master, Two-Gun-Pete from Texas, does a shooting act. We are the favourites. I hope you are not going to try and steal all the applause!"

I was nettled at this and tossed my head. "If people applaud me it will be because they like me," I answered.

"If my act is better than yours, of course I shall get the cheers."

"Well, keep away from me then," Bluegrass answered calmly. "I shall kick you if I feel like it."

"Now then, you two," said a little thin voice beyond the partition.

"Who's that?" I asked my companion.

"That is Delhi, the elephant!" Bluegrass blew thoughtfully into his hay. "He is very clever and gives us all good advice. Perhaps I will not kick you, after all."

I was very interested in the American horse, and he became more friendly and said that he would tell me some of his adventures. Towards evening an atmosphere of excitement grew so tense that it was almost painful. Men, dressed in wonderful, shiny clothes with sequins winking in the light, passed through our tents. Other men groomed and dressed the liberty-horses with jingling bridles all covered in flashing metal discs and with short plumes stuck in silver sockets and attached to their head-harnesses.

I could not help hoping that I too might wear something like this, and I felt I could hardly wait for the next evening. A band struck up in the distance and after that, until the circus finished at eleven, there was one constant whirl of coming and going, hoofs banging as horses backed against the wooden partitions, voices calling, encouraging or chiding, the snaky flash and cracks of the long whips which sounded threatening but which were never allowed to touch us. Clouds of dust rose suffocatingly and eddied round the swinging lanterns, so that their rays appeared to be darting through smoke-screens.

When it was all over and all was still again, with only one man sitting yawning on an upturned bucket and acting as night-watchman, Bluegrass told me something of his story.

"I was born and brought up on the prairie," he began, "and after the wonderful thrill of life out there all this seems very tame. I was the most famous bucking-bronco from Oklahoma to the Sierra Madre. I could buck anything off my back that tried to ride me, and all through the sheer joy of living. It gave me the greatest delight to come to grips with some of those men—and, mind you, they *could* ride! People over here don't know the meaning of the word. They think that a kind of rocking-chair gallop on a good-tempered old hunter is riding. My word, they wouldn't last two seconds on one of us Western fire-eaters."

"My master can ride too," I cried in hot indignation.

"Can he?" Bluegrass snorted doubtfully. "Let him get on my back tomorrow and we'll soon see. Well, to go on. Hop, skip and buck I would go, and jounce, bump, off they would come in the corral, and if they were lucky and I didn't tread on them on purpose maybe they'd get off with just bruises."

"I think that was pretty mean of you," I said, and was rather surprised at myself. "What was the good of behaving like that? You hadn't any grudge against them."

"Well, no," Bluegrass admitted. "I was quite fond of some of them and I knew they liked me. It was just—oh, that was how we did things on the Lazy K Ranch."

I was carried away by my feelings and I shook my head till my picket-rope slammed against the bucket. "If Andrea got on your back you couldn't buck him off," I boasted.

The American horse rolled an amused eye at me. "That, son, remains to be seen," he said. "If he stays on he'll be the first man that ever did once I began bucking. And I feel you ought to know how to buck, yourself; you never know, it might come in useful. You may not always have Andrea for a master and you may want to be rid of your rider some- time. Now, look at me. Put your feet so, like this, see?

Take a short, stiff jump, so, and come down *so*! That's it. Now, never forget that, son."

I promised that I would not and Bluegrass went on in a more dreamy tone, for it was late, the place was hushed, and we were all sleepy.

"Two-Gun-Pete was the only man I never tried to unseat. Why? I don't know—I just didn't. And *he* brought me to Europe and got us into this show and here I am. This is safer than riding after dry-gulchers with the Sheriff's posse thundering along or rounding up longhorns in the foothills. Well, you've got a big day before you, son. Maybe we'd better hit the straw now. So long!"

"So long!" I answered, using the strange expression that Bluegrass had let fall.

CHAPTER SEVEN

I RISE IN THE WORLD

I WAS soon asleep, but I had queer dreams of bucking off Andrea and treading on him, which made me groan and shiver in my sleep and kick feebly in the straw till its rustling woke me and I found the night-watchman regarding me suspiciously.

"Shurrup!" he advised shortly and went back once more to his bucket.

Next day they took me and rehearsed me in the empty gloom of the circus till Andrea and I were perfect and Melville expressed himself as delighted. Some of the other horses who had been exercising round the ring were standing about and I could see they were amazed at me.

I felt very proud of myself and quite pleased when I noticed Bluegrass's bulging eyes looking at me with new respect.

"You didn't say, son, that you were as educated as that," he said slowly, "and there I was shooting off my mouth teaching you how to buck and you knowing all *that* all the time. Why, I reckon I never saw anything to touch that counting stunt. But don't forget what I taught you; it might come in mighty useful one day!"

Little did I then think, in my young arrogance, of how and when I should be glad of that knowledge.

About six o'clock a groom came to prepare me. My coat was already as satin-soft as it was possible to make it, but the man was not satisfied and went over it again with a hay wisp till Andrea, who came at that moment to look after me, said: "Why, he's like a black mirror, Luke. If that's your standard I'm going to have my work cut out to keep Stardust up to it."

I hardly knew my young master, but I felt very proud of him. He was dressed from head to heels in sequin tights, over which he had a little leather bolero embroidered with blue stars, and a broad belt. On his feet were blue Morocco leather shoes. His head was bare, but his curly hair had been treated with some scented oily stuff so that the curls kept stiffly in place and might have been carved in buttered ebony.

Then they brought my things. They put a broad embroidered girth round my middle and a headstall and bridle with blue and gold stars on it over my head. Every move I made caused the stars to wink incessantly, and right on top between my ears was a wonderful floating plume.

Andrea leaped up on to my back to ride me into the ring, or rather just to this side of the entrance-curtain, where we waited out of sight for our cue. Somewhere just overhead a magnificent brass band was thumping and blaring away at a march-tune which made my feet prance with excitement. I felt Andrea touch me quietly on the neck.

"Take it easily, old boy," he whispered. "This is our great chance if we pull it off."

Then there was a lot of banging and shooting, for the turn before ours was Bluegrass and his Texan master. With a swish, two grooms drew back the curtain and Bluegrass came galloping out with Two-Gun-Pete waving his shooting-irons round his head and yelling like a wildcat. Just as he passed me he let off the final shot. It was too much. I reared with a snort of terror, and, as I stamped my hind feet in that soft, churned-up ground, I heard the band begin the slow dreamy music which they had played when we practised.

Had Andrea showed impatience then or tried to force me I never would have gone into the ring, for some queer fright had gripped me by the throat. But he laughed! Andrea, poising and balancing himself to my movements, just laughed, not maliciously but triumphantly, as if in delight at the spirit and temper of the animal he owned.

Human laughter has always had the strangest effect on me. It half scares, half worries and subdues me, for few animals can grasp the queerness of laughing. In a few seconds I was as calm and serene as if nothing could ever trouble me again. I dropped quietly back to earth and gave a little whinny as if to tell my young master that I would do my best.

He patted me again and next moment we had passed between the brocaded curtains and were in the dazzling crossbeams of the great lights trained on us. But I heard one of the grooms in the entrance say to the other: "There's gunpowder in that there horse, Bill. Don't you never do nothing to upset him. He's the kind what will hold a grudge for ten years and then trample on you if he got the chance. See his eye? I'd sooner ride old Bathsheba, the Malay tiger!"

Perhaps, of all the great moments in my life, the one that I love to remember best and that warms my old heart most was that moment when I had my first sight of the circus at night; in row upon row, right up to where the roof-arch began, were all those people. You could not pick out any one person, but just ring upon ring of pale faces like ox-eye daisies in a field. They were not still, but seemed to weave and sway as if swimming in dusty space, but this may have been a trick of the light or my own excitement.

For a moment there was silence, and then came the voice of the ringmaster—Melville himself—announcing us. Andrea pressed me with his knees and I walked forward carefully with the little mincing steps the other horses used. There was an expectant little attempt at clapping as if to encourage us, but it hushed quickly. We were new; no one had seen our turn; and no one was particularly impressed except by our spectacular appearance.

And then our act began, and the carefully prepared trick worked over and over again. At first they would not believe their eyes. Andrea slipped off my back to stand beside me and I pawed the ground to our signal. Again and again we were right.

Excitement began to mount and there were a few cries that it was a trick and that no animal could count. They were right, if they had only known it.

"Stand away from the Counting Arab," Melville commanded, though all this was prearranged too. "See, he is not touching the wonderful horse now. Now, may I have another number?"

"Thirty!" someone shouted.

I could see that the shiny-faced man was troubled. He had asked the audience at the start to keep below fifteen. I felt that somehow an awful lot depended on me and that in the next few minutes I could make Andrea very happy or very miserable. I was keyed-up and excited.

There were some cries of "shame" and "make it easier," but my master's head was up; his black eyes shone, and to me he had never looked so good. I was trembling now and sweating for fear I should betray his trust in me.

Then Andrea gave the signal and I began to paw the ground with firm, deliberate strokes. It was so quiet now that the shuffling noise I made was quite loud. A thrilling whimper of sound, regular as breathing, grew and mounted, beating like a pulse in time with me, and I knew that all those hundreds of people were counting with me.

Eight, nine, ten! You could feel the growing tension of feeling like a current growing stronger. Fifteen, sixteen!

"No, he can't do it," a woman in the front row gasped and I almost lost the game by starting and glancing at her, but I just saved myself and went on watching my master's hand. In such a long count there was the added danger that some of the public would get tired of watching me and look at him, and then, surely, someone would guess.

Twenty-five, twenty-six, twenty-seven! Dead silence now. They had stopped counting. Twenty-eight, twenty-nine, thirty! Andrea's hand stopped its slight signal and I stopped too, feeling quite done up.

Then a roaring cheer crashed out, with stamping and whistling and shouts and hoots of delight. Still trembling but happy in Andrea's happiness, I was led out and back to my place in the picket-line and there I was given a lovely supper, which I munched in quiet content.

So this was fame! I was great! I had given all that thrill and pleasure out there to all those people. My wonderful life of glamour and adventure had begun as I used to dream it would when I wandered through the summer lanes with Gipsy Jacko's caravan. As I recalled now the faces, simple, willing and patient, of his other horses, I felt a gentle contempt for them and a wonder that they too did not break out into the world.

Of course I had loved the wandering life with the dear, good gipsies—in fact, I was rather surprised to find I felt sad at the idea that they were somewhere out there in the night, pushing off on their endless journeyings without me to be their joy and pride. But this—this was much better, and they would be proud of me when they heard.

CHAPTER EIGHT

FAME AT LAST

WHEN THE performance reached half way, there was a pause, and quite a lot of the people came round to the back to see the animals. The grooms came to ring me round, but whether to guard me or the crowd I could not make out.

They need not have feared. I loved those people and their wonder and surprise. They patted me, some timidly, some boldly, and I pranced a little in my rustling straw to show I was pleased.

But it was the children that I loved best. Their little hot hands felt pleasant patting my chest and legs, for most of them could not reach much higher. I snorted softly and encouragingly through my nose and sidled and arched my neck when the grown-up men and women patted me, and the grooms said: "Take care, ma'am; careful, sir—the Arab's a queer-tempered beast."

But when the children loved me I put down my head and touched their little woolly clothes with my velvet nose, and they squealed in their delight.

Sometimes, as I got better known, they brought me gifts of food, sweet apples and nice brown crusts; if the groom said it was all right for me I ate them. Happy, wonderful days!

At night, Bluegrass and I often had long talks, and he had quite dropped his slightly contemptuous tone with me; he even asked now for my opinion from time to time.

He was still certain, however, that no horseman could compete with his Texan master, but he did not sneer quite so much at Andrea. My fame got about and soon there were long queues at each performance, and always the circus was packed each night. The "house full" board, painted up in big red letters on a white ground, was kept near the entrance and old Melville went about rubbing his big, broad palms together with a rough, dry sound and patting on the back all those whom he met.

On the rare occasions when I left the circus-grounds, I saw my picture on the huge bills posted on hoardings or hung in shop windows. You cannot really wonder that I felt as if all the world were at my feet. People would whisper and turn to stare after Andrea and me.

I remember that sometimes I saw, down town, horses who filled me with a curious, disdainful pity, for they had not become great or famous—they were not even as well off as Bob, the old white horse of my gipsy wandering days, for *he* had enough to eat, and fresh air and sunshine. But some of these creatures were in pitiable situations, drawing refuse-carts or heavy cabs. Their ribs often showed gauntly under their dirty coats, their eyes held the hopeless dullness of complete resignation. Somehow, I used to feel very sad when I saw them, even though I felt then that perhaps it was their own fault. I was always glad when I got back to the headlong excitement and glitter of the circus life with its music and happy atmosphere. I asked Bluegrass if there were poor horses in his country.

"Sure, there are everywhere, son," he said, stamping restlessly. "Man is not fair to us. Maybe someday they will invent machinery to do all the work we do so ungrudgingly today, and then we shall begin to come into our own, for we shall start dying out and becoming rare and man will take more care of the ones that are left. But that will not be in our time!"

I could not get Bluegrass's words out of my head for some time.

The weeks grew into months—winter passed and the circus prepared to go on the roads. The big-top was got out of storage, and such a polishing and working began as I could not have believed possible.

By this time, Andrea and I were the show-pieces of Melville's Circus and were the main item on the show-bills. Even Bluegrass and his Texan took second place now, but I must say he was quite nice about it.

But for the first time I began to regret my tremendous fame. *Now* I was never allowed to leave the grounds at all, but took my exercise wearily round and round the ring. As spring came it brought little change to the grey stones of the town, but well I knew how, in the open country, the blossoms would be drifting their petal snow in the April gales, how the rolling hills would be turning emerald-green with the thrusting through of the young growth. There was a corner in the circus grounds hard by the board-fence shutting out the main street, and here a tuft of leaves I knew so well had burst defiantly through, a lovely patch of colour on the dry grey earth. I watched that little clump, and when one day the acorn-shaped buds opened wide into pungent yellow dandelions I pranced excitedly at the memories they brought of open ways and unhemmed skies.

But I was guarded too well to have the chance I longed for of galloping breathlessly out again, away and free; men never left me lest someone should try to steal me or harm me, for there were plenty who were jealous of Melville's success. All this I learned from the grooms gossiping to the night-watchman on his bucket.

And now, as often as not, Andrea would bring a rug and make himself a straw bed near me for the night. One night he was sitting up with me because I was not feeling well. There was nothing really the matter with me—I was always in radiant health—but I had had a shock that day. The circus was going on the roads the next day and the big cats were being boxed. I had never been allowed anywhere near them and so had seen nothing of them. Indeed I had forgotten completely that queer smell which had upset me so when first their cage-cars had passed me in the procession. But now, unavoidably, I came up against them.

I had been exercised in the open field at the back, if a dry dust waste can earn the name of field, and as I was led back I had to pass two big cages about to be hauled up the wooden ramp on to a car. I stopped and began to shake with a strange cold feeling which froze me as if I were a stone horse. I felt my nostrils open wide and I am sure my eyes were ringed with white. All I could see in the gloom of that cage were the topaz eyes watching in unwinking malice.

The hot, cat smell suffocated me and I shook and sweated as I stood there. The groom leading me was one whom I did not know very well, so when he chirruped to me to come on I had no confidence, but strained against his hold and began to stamp with my forefeet.

"Stardust!" It was Andrea's voice shouting to me as he ran up. "Come with me! Leave go, fellow. I'll take him!" He came between me and the cage cutting off with his body that malignant, speculative stare. Something seemed to snap in me and I stopped trembling and followed Andrea humbly back to my place, rubbing my face against his shoulder to thank him.

But I suffered for the shock, as would all highly strung animals. They had to cut my performance that night, and even from where I was I could hear the stamping and roaring of the disappointed crowd. I was very much frightened and Andrea said he would sit up with me.

That was how I first heard about the men's suggestion that my young master should try to ride Bluegrass. They were all talking together while the American horse and I were

having our last sweet mouthfuls of hay. Two-Gun-Pete
was attending to Bluegrass, and he turned and looked at
me.

"Waal, if I didn't hev my own mount, brother," he said,
laughingly, "I wouldn't mind heving yourn, and that's sure
the highest praise I can give."

"Of course, I'm prejudiced." Andrea smiled quietly as he
spoke. "But I don't echo your thought. I want no horse but
Stardust, do I, pal?" And he slapped me in friendly delight.

"That's understandable," said the night-watchman, grin-
ning all over his face, while I looked in dismay at Bluegrass,
fearing something awful—sensing what was coming. Even
the American horse seemed worried and tossed his head up
and down as if to ease himself. "Understandable," the man
said again, "because he can ride your mount, Andrea, for a
cert, but you could not mount on his."

There was such a silence that I could hear a cricket as it
ran along over the floor, its long feelers waving for crumbs
from the men's sandwiches. Then my young master spoke
up.

"Who says I can't ride Bluegrass?" he asked, almost
wonderingly, and one of the men gasped.

"Come, ye can't, son," he answered, almost sharply, perhaps thinking to stop this dangerous talking before it went
too far. He could not, of course, have used a more dangerous
line of reasoning. "That horse is an American bucking devil
—a real Wild West horror. Yes, of course, you don't know.
You've never seen anyone but Two-Gun-Pete up and
he's the only man Bluegrass won't send flying and then roll
on."

"That remains to be seen," Andrea said calmly. He was
patting me all the time he spoke and there was not a tremor
in his touch. "Pete, if you'll lend me Bluegrass early tomorrow I'll see whether or no he is as bad as you say."

"He's all that, brother," Pete said earnestly. "I kinda don't want you to do this. I reckon it's murder, and what's to become of Stardust when you're crippled and can't never ride again?"

"Come, don't hang me yet," Andrea bantered. "Stardust shall feel me on his back again many and many a time."

"Not if you try this crazy stunt," Pete answered gloomily. "And they'll all say I arranged it to get even with you for ousting me on the bills."

"We're witness for you that it wasn't so," said the watchman eagerly.

I could hardly believe my ears, or my eyes as I looked at all their faces. They *wanted* the test to come off. It was an exciting suggestion; they looked forward to the battle of strength that it would mean. It would be such a complete change from routine. If only men would set their ambitions on more worthy aims! Andrea was as eager as they were. I could tell it in the glow on his cheeks and the flash in his dark eyes.

I felt sick with fear for him. There was a bond between us, wrought strangely from our wanderings together, and I think he knew at once that I was troubled. He stroked and patted me and then took to warming my velvet ears between his hands, for they were miserably cold.

After he had warmed and comforted me I felt better, but when they had settled the details and all was quiet again, with Andrea asleep on his rug, heedless of tomorrow, I talked far into the night with Bluegrass.

"Don't buck him off," I begged the American horse.

He shook himself gloomily. "It's no good," he said. "I shall do as I always have done. If he is man enough to stick on I'll not complain. I'd rather it were he—I tell you straight —than any of the riders I have ever known, bar Two-Gun-Pete. But if I didn't try you'd know he hadn't won fairly and you'd always remember it and so would I. But why man can't leave well alone I don't know. Stupid blundering children, that's what they are, colts who will never grow up, whom no harness of fate can discipline out of their own foolish little strivings for applause!"

CHAPTER NINE

ANDREA'S GREAT FIGHT

I SHALL never forget that night. I could not sleep a wink, and my imagination painted such pictures that I was soon in a dreadful state, and began swishing my long tail, the warning sign of a coming kick. But it was no good lashing out. I was helpless and this feeling made it worse.

Cool dawn-winds came rustling over the circus grounds, rolling the empty paper bags over the hard earth. There was a lot of whispering and talking, because not one of those men wanted old Melville to hear, for if he had realised what was going on he would soon have stopped it.

There was an open piece of softer ground behind the tents of the liberty-horses, and here they decided to hold the trial. I could see quite well from my lines, for near me the canvas was being taken down to be packed up and I had a clear view.

Bluegrass was led out, swishing his tail and rolling his eyes and apparently in an evil temper. He said he'd been put in a spot, whatever he meant by that, and I could not help being rather sorry for him. But I could only give him a passing thought. All my life seemed to be bound up in Andrea. I never could have believed that I should so have cared for anyone besides myself. By this time I no longer cared whether he succeeded or no, whether they cheered or booed him, only so long as the bright life could go on shining in him and his fine brave body remain unbroken.

Two men were holding Bluegrass and it took all their strength. It did not help me to see that one of them was Two-Gun-Pete himself, looking palely anxious as if now he was regretting his part in the stupid attempt. Bluegrass I hardly recognised at all. I had never seen him look like this. He bared his lips off his long white teeth and he kicked and kicked till the ground became churned up with his struggles. It was terrifying to see that he took no notice even of what Pete said to him. Some dreadful temper seemed to have woken in him after a long, long sleep.

"Mount him eff you're going to, brother!" Pete gasped. "We can't hold him much longer." Andrea vaulted on to the bronco's back and the two men leaped back and scurried to the shelter of some crates, behind which the other men had taken cover.

Bluegrass stood quite still for the space of five seconds— no longer. In that brief space my young master put out all his strength to get the grip he wanted on his horse. Then Bluegrass began. He did everything a horse can do except climb up the broad fence into the street, and as he looked then in his evil, flashing mood I don't think that anyone would have been surprised if he had.

The splitting force of his dreadful bucks were enough to shake a man's eyes loose in his head. He reared and pawed at the air, and I looked to see Andrea use the same hold he had on me, but no—he had no time, no breath for it; all his energy and skill must be used in hanging on to this mountain of seeming steel and rubber. I could hardly believe my eyes and I neighed shrilly to him in my terror and dismay.

His face, white under its habitual tan, stared unseeingly; deep lines had appeared beside his tightly shut mouth. Blood was beginning to run from his nose and still that pitiless bucking went on and on.

But—Andrea was still mounted on the bronco's back! A low mutter of excitement began to grow into subdued shoutings of encouragement. Two-Gun-Pete had tossed his stetson on the ground and was jumping on it in the abandonment of his excitement. To do him justice, he was as pleased as anyone that so far the gipsy had made good his boast. Even Bluegrass seemed surprised that he still had a rider. His nostrils were wide open and blood-red, his eyes were shocking to see, but—and I almost fell over when I realised it—Bluegrass was tiring too!

He had forgotten and the men had all forgotten that it was six long years since he had left the States behind, and the bloom of youth's supreme strength was no longer on him. Bluegrass would go on exerting every ounce of energy he possessed until either he vanquished Andrea or broke his own magnificent heart. Submission was completely out of his reckoning.

I think that Andrea, with his wonderful gipsy's under-standing of horses, sensed exactly how it was with Blue-grass. His mouth was grimly set as ever, but he was tired to death and so was the American horse. Man and bronco, they were killing each other.

And then Andrea was off and rolling swiftly out of reach of those wicked feet. With bared teeth, Bluegrass was after him, but five men, who were to be commended for their pluck, raced across and caught him and held him. After the first second they had no difficulty.

His head drooping, his flanks heaving and shiny with sweat, on which the whirling dust was settling like hoar-frost, Bluegrass stood shaking like a leaf. He was coughing too in a sad little strained kind of way. But I craned my neck to look after Andrea.

They gathered him up and laid him on the crates, and I was sure he was dead. He lay as still as the stone images in quiet graveyards round tree-shadowed churches. The men were working over him, and three of them were leading away the foam-covered American horse, when everyone whirled round at the sound of a familiar voice, to stand petrified, for there was old Melville himself. Only today his face was not shining with good temper but black anger. He said nothing at first, but there was that in the withering scorn of those hard, bead-like eyes which made the men hang their heads, ashamed of their childish folly. He pointed, and his gesture woke them once more into action, so that they slunk away. Only one man had the hardihood to remain beside Andrea's senseless body and face the owner's bleak displeasure, and that was Pete.

Melville crossed over and stood glooming down at them. Then in an awkward way he picked up the limp brown wrist to feel for the pulse. Then he spoke.

"I suppose he deserved to have broken his neck playing the donkey like that, but he's alive. Get him to his quarters. He'll not be in the ring tomorrow night at our new pitch, that's one certain thing. They'll wreck my big top for sure when they know, the people. He didn't think of that in his selfish pride!"

And saying no more, he stalked away. I watched the men return and help Pete carry Andrea away and I was in a tumult of emotions. Relief and love for my young master mingled with doubts of the future. I now saw something I had never realised before: evil results from our own rash actions don't all fall on ourselves—it might be better if they did. Others get hurt too and we can't stop that. Now, out of all this foolish boasting might well come disaster if the public, disappointed as they had been before, tried to wreck things in their chagrin. If anything awful happened, as I had heard tell of when wandering shows travelled in the wilder northern counties, many innocent people would get hurt.

It was a new lesson for me from the hard book of life. Then and there I felt the first twinge of regret that I had ever wanted to come out of my security to seek success among men.

CHAPTER TEN

THE FIRST PARTING

THAT morning we got away, and now I, too, was in the great procession I had watched that winter's day. But much of the glamour and romance were gone from it all for me.

I had not seen Andrea again and I was in a fret of worry so that I would eat nothing. Bluegrass too seemed to have disappeared, so perhaps he did the journey in one of the cars, for he must have been pretty well "used up", to employ his own phrase.

The only consolation to me was that once more I saw and smelled the lovely countryside, heard the bleating of sheep and little lambs, and the chuckle of little streams tumbling over their stony beds in the woodlands. We passed an apple-orchard, and the heady sweetness distilling on the quiet air made my heart ache with longing for something I did not understand.

Then into the bustle and hum of a big town again, and all went at their work with a will. Ropes tautened and the big top rose mushroom-like from the field grass. Straw was heaped for the animals, trapezes were set up, bench planks were unpacked and hurried into position, so that from nothing there grew a warm, lighted palace of excitement and adventure with music and thrills where before had been only the drowsy buttercups.

Then I met Bluegrass again in our old familiar pickets. He was very moody, picking over his oats. As for me, I could touch nothing.

"I have been dreadfully worried about you," I said,

looking at him in wonder, for the Bluegrass I knew had changed somehow. There was a look of depression about him and a drooping air in the way he stood. I asked him how he felt, but he only kicked out in a spiritless kind of way as if from mere habit.

"Beaten," he said hollowly, "beaten by a boy, a gipsy-boy! I, Bluegrass, who have thrown some of the best men of the West!"

I felt bewildered and stupid. "But," I said, "what do you mean? You were not beaten, although I do think that it took you longer than you had expected."

Bluegrass rolled a dejected eye round at me. "I'm good for nothing now," he said. "I shouldn't be surprised if they sold me for hounds' meat any day. Beaten—of course I was beaten! I didn't unseat Andrea. He fell off deliberately!"

I couldn't think; my head was whirling. "Why, oh, why? He could have won, could have made all those mockers look so silly."

"Because——" Bluegrass spat out some of his food viciously. "Because he *knew*! Gipsies always know. They, of all peoples in the world, can read our minds. He knew that I should die rather than give in, and I must say I nearly did. I was so exhausted that I couldn't even see for the last half minute. So he ended it deliberately to save me because he liked my pluck. He'd won enough laurels to show that it didn't only take an American to hold in a bucking horse and he was content to leave it at that. But I wish he'd killed me! I shall never live down this feeling of shame at sight of him!"

I may say here that Bluegrass was putting some of this on; he did live it down and regained most of his old hardy spirits, but he was never known to buck again.

As for me, I felt such a glow of pride and joy that all my appetite came rushing back and I made a hearty meal at last. Things went off better than Melville had expected and the tents were not wrecked, although there was much trouble and grumbling and many people demanded their money back—and got it.

Next morning, Andrea came to me and put his arms round me as he used to do, and loved me.

"There were times when I was on that brute," he whispered, "when I never expected to be able to do this again."

I nosed against him and he laughed and pulled my ears and I felt that a very bad patch in our lives was over. We went into the ring again that night, and if our success before had been great, now it was overwhelming. People stood up on the benches and screamed at us, and many of them threw money into the ring; this the clowns picked up and carried to Andrea. Melville cheered and the grooms cheered, and the band beat at their big drums as if they had suddenly gone quite mad.

I felt very happy, and I had a bran-mash that night. I said to myself that the world was, after all, a very good place. But dark clouds of events were rolling up on my horizon and I had not many more months of circus life to enjoy. But through the long summer days we visited many places and gave so many performances that we often made headlines in the evening papers.

Andrea taught me some other very clever tricks, but none was quite so popular as the counting. When winter came we made our way back to the town and the brick-built building we had used before. It was here that the first break came in our long line of successes.

How well I recollect every little detail of that night. It was late January of a mild winter, when warm rains had bogged the country roads all through a hot November, when fogs rolled through the streets, making the lamps look like oranges suspended in space. Everyone was restless and out of sorts, even the animals. Often I listened to low grumbling whines coming from the big cats' quarters, which had, for some reason, been arranged more on this side of the camp-site. Each time I heard it I shook, and with head up and eyes wide with fear strained against my picket-rope.

Horses often suffered dreadfully because their instinct is to gallop away from what scares them, as, ages long gone by, they galloped on the grassy plains before man came. But in service as we are we cannot fly, and it is very terrifying.

Well, on this particular night it was raining, as usual. Long queues of people stood patiently waiting for the ticket-office—usually arranged in one of our cars—to open. They were all so wet and draggled that it did not make much difference getting a little wetter, and, anyway, no doubt they knew that once inside they would forget all troubles and discomforts, taken out of themselves into a world of tinsel and glamour.

As they filed in and began shuffling along the rows, I heard Luke say to one of the grooms: "Nero is restless. I wish they'd keep him out of the ring-cage tonight. Don't know what ails him, unless it is the weather. That'd be enough to give a saint the hiccups." There was a laugh, and then they moved away. Nero was the biggest of the lions and usually good and tractable, but he was uncertain. One day he'd fawn on you and next day try and knock you down, or so his trainer said.

I hated to hear even his name, for the very word, lion, had an odd effect on me. Pete on Bluegrass came bounding between the curtains, and it was our turn. I was so used by this time to the crushing applause that always greeted us that I never noticed it but pricked daintily into the ring, pleased and happy to feel that everyone there was eager to see me and be pleased at what I could do. They would cheer and

c

cheer at the very sight of us, we had become so well known. Often Melville had to blow his whistle and hold up his hands to quieten them before he could make himself heard announcing our act.

It was the same tonight, but above the roar of the cheers I was certain I heard another roar, quite a different sound, full of menace and hate. I knew that my ears pricked forward and back in a frenzied effort to locate the direction.

"He's out; Nero's loose," I heard a man shout and I felt Andrea stiffen in the saddle, so I knew he had heard too. The worst was that not only had he heard but so had most of the people seated near the place at the side where the lions' entrance-tunnel was placed.

They rose like a cresting wave and hung on the verge of a panic stampede for the open, afraid of the unknown, afraid of being shut in the circus with a lion on the run. Nero was no longer to them a pleasant thrill—a part of the performance to which they had looked forward eagerly. He was what he had always been under his veneer of training, a jungle animal ready to defend itself in its own jungle way. And these people didn't want a jungle animal. Suddenly, they all wanted to be a long way off.

Melville walked into the ring. I could not help admiring him. In his place I should have wanted to run, but he knew that it would calm everyone if they saw him saunter into the ring unconcernedly.

"Stay where you are, good people," he shouted cheerfully. "Nothing's wrong. They've had a little trouble with Nero, our tame old lion, but he's in his cage all right. You sit tight and let us go on entertaining you. That's better; that's a lot better!"

He waved to the crowd, resettling themselves for all the world like a flock of starlings, startled when feeding on an autumn stubble-field. I learned afterwards, from the grooms' chatter, that he had to take a risk. Nero was *not* back in his cage at all, but Melville hoped he soon would be. The chances were that no harm would come from him, as the men would soon catch him if unhampered.

But if the crowd had stampeded many people would have been killed, especially children. Whether he was right or wrong in what he did is not for me to say. All I know is that it didn't help *me*!

To my keen nose was wafted the hot, pungent smell I had grown to fear and hate and I knew that Nero was prowling somewhere and watching me. It was no good. I began to shake and sweat as I always did and I could do nothing to stop it. Melville announced us and cracked his long whip. He was a brave man, for he did not know where Nero was and he couldn't go to see or help until he'd got our act going, or people would notice and the panic would mount again.

But as soon as he had barked out his introduction he slipped quietly away and Andrea began. I don't suppose I shall ever forget the feeling of shame and distress which seared me as I knew that I could not do my part. The queer hypnotism which the lion's presence always worked on me gripped me now, numbing my mind and paralysing my legs. I literally could not move. I was really and truly scared stiff, to use one of Bluegrass's expressions. I was cold down to my pasterns.

"Give the Counting Arab a number," Andrea called pleasantly to the crowd, and they now noticed nothing wrong. But I, who knew every tone of my loved master's voice, knew that he was putting a force on himself, guessing Melville's ruse. This scared me more than ever.

"Six," called out a weedy-looking old lady in the half-crown seats. We always tried to do our best turns just in front of the half-crown seats, so that those who had paid the higher prices should feel they were having their money's worth.

"Six it shall be," Andrea said. "Now watch the Counting Arabian. Come, Stardust, count it out."

He had slipped from my back and warned me to begin, but I rolled anguished eyes at him, for I could not move. The lion-smell was stronger than ever; I was petrified and coldly sick.

"Stardust!" There was a ringing note of command in Andrea's voice, but nothing could break the spell. He came over to me and patted me, thinking perhaps that with his hand upon me I should remember my part. Did he think that I had forgotten? No, I think he knew what was wrong, but he thought that I could break it if I tried.

"Count up to six," he said and pressed me lightly with his hand. Someone in the audience tittered. One waggish lout called out that I'd left my ready-reckoner at home. Then two or three more began to laugh. A little sizzle of merriment crisped along the rows like a first wave running over sun-baked sand.

"Stardust, don't let me down," Andrea whispered in pleading agony, and I began to tremble in my misery, for I could not help him. I could only stare with anguished eyes straining into the dark shadows beyond the side-door curtains, which were half pulled back. I was certain that I should see those topaz moons swim into view.

The crowd was taking it well, which was a good thing, for they might so easily have turned nasty.

"Go back to school," one cried, and then there was another burst of laughing.

"Get him out, Andrea." Melville's voice sounded near me as he hurried back. "Everything always goes wrong together, but they've caged Nero, thank heaven! Now get him out and hurry in the next turn before they begin throwing things!"

Ah, if he'd only known, it was not impossible even now

to retrieve matters. At his words, and more than that, the confident tone in which he spoke—so different from his first announcement that Nero was caged—I knew that it was really all right. I could have done my trick now, done it perfectly, but it was too late. As feeling flowed back into my cramped limbs I swayed in movement, thinking to paw the ground in my old trick, but Andrea was leading me out and it was all over.

I think he was as distressed as I, for he stayed by me, rubbed me down, put on my night-rugs, and fondled me. I could see by the look in his eyes that he was terribly sorry for me, but even he could not quite understand my terror of the big cats. But I had no fever and I ate my supper and relished it now that the trouble was over.

Melville himself came and stood by. "What was it, Andrea? First time I ever heard of a horse having a temperament. But it won't do. I'll take him off the bills for a while until this little failure blows over. If we were to baulk again they'd never forget it."

"Yes, sir," Andrea said miserably, for he was so fond of me.

Well, that was the end of my career as a famous circus horse. By the time I had rested for a few weeks and they were going to try again something happened to part my master and me. As my fame was a little dimmed they did not guard me quite so closely and I was even allowed a little liberty. Coming back to the circus-grounds one night after a pleasant ride out under the February stars we saw a sight I shall never forget. In a sheltered corner of a field where that day the farm-hands had been digging leeks for market now stood five big cars, a gipsy encampment. How it wakened old memories of happy colthood days! The acrid smell from the camp-fires from which the pale-blue smoke-wisps wavered upwards made me start and hesitate.

"Ah, ha, old fellow, that talks of home!" Andrea whispered hungrily and there was a quiver in his voice. Gipsy blood would out, and for weeks no doubt he had been unconsciously pining for the life he had known. But now with realisation of what he had missed his longing surged up impatiently, sweeping away all considerations of money-making or rising to greatness in the townsman's-world. The halter and the picket-rope, the wheel-track of a wandering caravan, the stamped-out fire as the dawn trek began, these things were the sap and joy of life. He reined me in, then turned into the field.

"Hail, there!" His ringing voice brought the brown-faced men and comely women to the doors. "What news of Gipsy Jacko and Brown Joan? I am Andrea, their son—Andrea, owner of Stardust!"

The leader nodded, taking a short black pipe from between his white teeth. "The same! They are at Norrington, two days to the west of here. Brown Joan has not left her caravan these four months past."

"Ah!" It was just one long-drawn-out quiver of a sigh from Andrea. Then he gripped me so hard with his knees, not realising what he did, that I shifted and pranced. "Steady old boy," he said to me. Then to the man: "Are you going on there?"

"By the dawn light."

"Then take this word: I am coming!"

Next moment we were galloping madly back towards the town. Never in all my life had Andrea ridden me so hard. He seemed not to care whether he broke his neck or I broke my legs. We thundered through the mean little streets on the outskirts of the town, scattering the alley-cats out scavenging in the lanes. We woke shattering echoes of drumming hoofs, so that in more than one window the lights sprang up to glow golden with blacked-out shapes against them where people crowded to see out and try to find out what madman was going by.

When we reached the circus I was flecked with foam and my flanks heaved. Andrea led me to my place and attended to me, but for once his mind seemed far away and I had a strange deserted feeling.

Bluegrass watched us in sedate surprise and when Andrea had done and hurried away in the direction of the boss's quarters he cocked a knowing eye at me.

"He's leaving," he snorted when I'd explained. "He'll never perform under the lights again. That's the worst of gipsy blood. They never settle. Hem them in with brick walls and tiled roofs, put money in their pockets and broadcloth on their backs, and one whisper of the forest-leaves under a crisping frost, one sight of the tracery of trees against a lemon sky, and the madness is in them and off they go. Is he taking you with him? I shall be sorry to lose you."

There was real feeling in Bluegrass's tones and in all my unhappiness I was grateful for this. But I had a big shock coming to me. Much later that night in the hush of the small hours Andrea crept to my side to say goodbye. I could not believe it. The desire to be understood by humans, to be able to talk to them, which is often such a gnawing pain of longing to us whom man rightly calls dumb beasts, was torture that night.

I rubbed my face against his sleeve, longing to hear him say he'd changed his mind. Oh, why did he not say that I too could go—could leave this life I hated now? But he said hardly anything at all. He stood for ages with one arm flung over my back while with the other hand he stroked and stroked my face. At last he roused himself with a deep sigh.

"Don't forget me, Stardust. I think it is better as it is. You'll go far in life. You have blue blood in you. Goodbye!"

He kissed me in a way he had never done before and then he was gone, but my velvet nose was wet with his tears. From stable-gossip in days to come I found that Andrea knew he would need a lot of money to look after Brown Joan in her declining years, and he had no option but to sell me. Melville paid well for me, the boy's most valuable possession. I tried to believe that I should see him again in the morning, but the echo of his voice was still, and for me the world was empty.

CHAPTER ELEVEN

THE PAINTING LADY

I THINK I date the beginnings of a lot of my troubles from that moment. No one understood me as he had done, though I must in fairness say that Melville's Circus was a very good one, that the animals were loved and well cared for, and that they enjoyed their life.

But there was no bond between me and the man who took over Andrea's act. We practised for some time together, but I could not shake off the nervousness left in me by the memory of Nero's break for freedom.

Sometimes I was so jumpy when I had to enter the ring that I fumbled my act badly, but for a long time the audiences remained loyal to me on the strength of past successes. It was not all my fault. Ryan, my new master, was not nearly as quick or clever as Andrea and often gave me my signal just too soon or too late, so that I was wrong in my numbers.

I could see that Melville was growing dissatisfied. I had ceased to be quite such a draw and I heard that he was advertising me for sale, for he knew that I ought to fetch nearly three times the sum which he had given Andrea. This news did not make me less nervous; every person who came round to look at the horses was to me of acute interest as he or she might well be my future owner.

And day after day I fretted for Andrea. I took little interest in my food, for everything seemed flavourless to me. I pined and lost weight. Sometimes I thought that I heard his step, and, oh, what a rush of joy I felt, so that my blood began to pound! But it was never his footfall, after all, and in my bitter disappointment I would lay my ears back threateningly.

One day, just before the afternoon performance, I saw with surprise that Melville himself was coming to inspect us. There was nothing strange in *that*, for he believed in personal attention to every detail of his big job, but it was an unusual time for him to come. With him was a lady, and she kept stopping and patting the horses and talking to them as if she liked them. She was not in the least afraid of us. She gazed with loving interest at Bluegrass, and he held his head down to her outstretched hand and nibbled her gloves in play as if he knew her. I think he was rather flattered that she stopped by him, for even the men took no liberties with the bronco, such was his reputation. This calm-eyed stranger seemed to take it for granted that she was safe. Then she turned to me.

"This is the horse, Miss Marsh," Melville said. "He's too good for us—he'll only play ball when he thinks, which is no good for me. I fancy he needs much more exercise than he gets here. What do you think of him?"

She did not answer all at once, but stood looking at me, and all at once I wanted to go with her. If I could not have Andrea and my old life of glamorous thrills, then I felt that it was far better to get right away. I thought, perhaps, that I might be happy with her. Young colts will notice that I craved fame no longer. I had lost something I valued, and now that it was gone I looked more humbly than I had ever done for a little happiness.

There was something lovely and strange about this lady and I believe the fascination lay in her eyes. She had a gentle, earnest way of looking at you, as if, for the moment, you were the thing that mattered most to her in all her life.

"Stardust," she said, and her voice matched her eyes. "What a nice name! Did you call him that?"

Melville laughed as he stroked his boot with his cane. "The gipsies called him that, ma'am. Somehow I respect the gipsies. I wouldn't change a name they had given!"

"I wouldn't, either," she said. "I like you, Stardust, and I'm going to buy you for myself."

Melville appeared uneasy, for he was a just and honest man. "Pardon me, but I thought it was for your brother, ma'am. I can hardly—you see, he's never been ridden except by men!"

I could not help thinking of Mrs. Farmer Dowling as he said this.

"He's a nervy animal and very high-spirited. I can't recommend him for you!"

Nina Marsh turned and smiled at Melville and she shook her head. She had wonderful hair, the colour of beech-trees in autumn, and any movement seemed to make sunny little flashes among the curls.

"It's no good arguing when I have made up my mind," she said softly. "You advertised him for sale and I intend to buy him, so that's that! I'm starting for Suffolk next month, so we can come to some arrangement, I know. I'll pay for you to keep him till then, and then send him to this address. Is that all right?"

Evidently it had to be, for Melville made no more comments, and, after a last loving pat, the lady walked away, her silky, dove-coloured dress rustling as it brushed against the trusses of straw which Luke had just brought in.

"*You're* in luck," Bluegrass grunted to me, banging his hoof against his drinking-bucket as he turned his head to look after her. "She's been here before, but not in your time. She paints pictures and once she came to do a series of circus pictures. There she sat, right in the middle of us

all, with her easels and brushes, and never turned a hair
even when the elephant picked up her box of colours in his
trunk thinking the bright tubes were good to eat. She used
to bring us lovely treats, and all of us, from the old man
down to the performing dog, were sorry when she packed up
and went on to another job somewhere else."

You can imagine that the next few weeks could not pass
quickly enough for me. I wanted to get away from haunting
memories of Andrea and try to start life afresh. My spirits
rose at the thought of going into the country, for one of our
grooms was a Suffolk man, and from his talk I gathered that
the country was very beautiful.

At last the day came, a fine day in late spring. Spring
always seems to me a time full of hope. I longed to be off.
Bluegrass said goodbye moodily, and I could see he felt
more than he would allow.

"Of course we shall miss you," he said testily. "The place
won't seem the same ever! You've waked us all up, you
and your precious Andrea, and brought a bit of life and
excitement into the place, and now you go skulking off just
when it suits you. Unfair, I call it. I'm going to be
thoroughly miserable, but nobody cares. I daresay I shall
bite my groom—the way I feel at the moment. You were
always different from us; you were even a cut above the
liberty-horses, though I never told you, as you were con-
ceited enough without that. There, go on and get away
before I say too much!"

Luke came at this moment to lead me away and that was
the last time I ever saw Bluegrass. I gazed back with wistful
affection at the old circus buildings, at the exercise-ground
and the board-fence where my dandelions grew. Melville
was standing to see me go, and most of the men, but the
man who mattered to me the most, where was he?

Luke took me to the station and handed me over to a man

who was there waiting for me and who got me into my box on the train—not without a good deal of stamping and resistance on my part, for he never explained what he wanted, but just pushed me and jerked at my mouth in a maddening way as if he was out of temper.

I tossed my head in the air and snatched at everything within reach till big flecks of white foam began to dabble my sides. If it had not been for a kindly old porter, used to boxing horses for Newmarket, who came and gave the right kind of assistance, they would never have got me up that sloping ramp, which in itself was terrifying.

When at last I was secure, I felt hot, frightened and quite out of sorts. The motion was trying, too, a swaying, banging kind of travelling which took me by surprise just when I was getting used to it, so that I felt unsafe on my feet. I was tired and thirsty and I had no one to talk to and nothing to comfort me. Andrea had never failed to understand me, to know all my needs almost before I did. It seemed to be an instinct in him. No one could be less like him than Rice Barsard, the new groom. He looked as if at some time in his life he had been passed through a wringer which had squeezed every bit of life-juice out of him, leaving only a tough, fibrous kind of man with skin the colour of a drowned slug. His eyes were the only things that appeared alive about him, and they were of that quick, shifty variety that saw every fault and ugly thing in life, and seemed to pierce it and hold it up to view as if they had been two needles instead of eyes.

I just didn't *like* Rice Barsard from the first and I was determined that I would resist any unfair treatment of his even if it meant rearing and kicking.

That was a long, weary afternoon. No one brought me anything to eat even when we had some time to wait on sidings. The train continued to bang and grind along. I think, of all creatures, horses need a companion most. A lonely horse is a very sad thing and will be glad of even a dog or cat to chum up with if there are none of his own kind about. There was no one to whom I could turn for comfort or advice, and so I stood there on tired feet, rocking slightly with the strange motion, dispirited, hungry and sore.

Presently the air changed and became cooler where it entered my prison through chinks and cracks. I snuffed eagerly, for I had not tasted that fresh sweetness in the air for nearly seven years. It was the smell of salt, the wind off the open sea billowing in over the cornlands of the East Coast, as I used to smell it when the Channel gales swept inland in those first weeks of my life.

At long, long last, with a good deal of shunting and crashing, my car was shot on to a siding and came to rest. I was thankful, for the motion had made me feel very queer indeed. Someone came and rolled back the doors and I stared out. It was a refreshing sight. All about us was the gentle inaction of a country station between trains. Rows of sedate churns winked in the sunset-light. The early summer blooms in the garden-strip under the office windows were nodding gaily, ballrooms for the bees who were dancing over them.

Barsard came for me, and because I wanted very much to get out managed to get me clear with no trouble. He led me out into a sandy lane and I followed meekly enough, for I was anxious to reach my new home and get some supper and rest.

CHAPTER TWELVE

HARD TIMES

THE first sight of that cottage in Suffolk was as cheering as a lark's song. So low was the thatched roof that the honeysuckle struggling over it could be picked while a person stood by the nail-studded front door. Tall tulips could nod on a level with the window-sills, but no one could see in despite the low windows, for the centuries-old bottle-glass let in light but no vision.

Nina Marsh was standing there in the evening light and her face was aglow with pleasure. But a quick frown settled as we got nearer, though it was a puzzled frown. Loving horses and painting them, she had very little knowledge of their care and management, and was shocked by my jaded appearance while not understanding it.

"What's the matter with Stardust?" she asked Barsard shortly. "He looks miserable."

The man touched his cap respectfully, but there was a distinctly contemptuous leer about him as he answered.

"Ah, that's nothing, lady. A train-journey's bound to upset a horse the first time he tries it. He'll be all right after a night's sleep."

She came and patted me, but I was too weary to respond much, though I arched my neck and tried to show I was pleased and grateful. But my stable round at the back of the cottage was snug—almost too snug. It had an un-ventilated smell about it and I was completely alone.

As I munched my hay I could hear nothing but the tapping of a branch against the panes of the loft-window and the chirping of the crickets. All my life I had spent with other horses about me, and in the circus days had always been surrounded by life and noise. The heavy quality of the quietness hanging in the air as if it were a thick curtain got on my nerves. But I should have been used to it soon enough and got off to sleep if it had not been for something else.

I first noticed the little scurrying sounds as I finished my meal and then I saw the lean, grey shapes of countless rats loping along their own runs, through and over the straw, along the beams and wall-ledges. Their sinuous galloping run and the occasional bickerings as they disputed passage with each other was a revel which I could see was to go on all night. As long as they kept away from me I could stand it, no doubt. They were not the first rats I had seen, but I had never seen so many all together and when I had nothing else to distract me. I found later that there was an immense mill-pond on the other side of the cottage and on its banks was a very citadel of rats undisturbed for years, as the cottage had stood empty a long time.

But the rats were curious and soon they came to have a look at me and sniff round my feet. This I just could not bear and I lashed out, hoping to discourage them. There were muffled squeals and scamperings and then quiet—for a time. But soon they were back, and again I kicked in desperate hopes of routing them. Rats about my feet I hate with a deep, instinctive dread which I cannot explain.

I don't think I hit any rats, but my steel shoes drummed on the partition woodwork with a sonorous bang which echoed into the night. Again and again I kicked and I did not care a rap if I hit that partition, for even the noise was some company to me, so low was my state.

After I had kept this up for some time, I heard steps coming from the little hut which Barsard had taken for himself. I also heard women's voices from the house where Nina and her little maid stood at the lighted window and called out.

"What is it, Rice? Why is he kicking?"

"Temper, lady, just vicious temper," I heard the man reply. He was muttering angrily as he flung open the stable-door. From the sweetness of the spring night air which breathed in I could guess how stale was the atmosphere about me. "Stop that racket, you brute!" Barsard said and came into the place, his thin figure making a wand-like shadow on the floor to skip ahead of him. He had a heavy stick in his hand and his fingers were working along it as if feeling for the best grip. He lunged forward and hit me over the head twice. No man had ever struck me like that before! All the fighting blood of a long-gone ancestry who had had to battle for their life surged up hotly in me. I had not dreamed I could feel like this.

Before I knew what I had done I had wheeled round and stretched out my neck, teeth bared as I had seen Bluegrass bare his. If I had caught the man's shoulder as I meant to do, I should have crushed the bone.

He leaped back with a curse and stumbled out of reach. "If that's your game I'll match you," he shouted and dived for a driving whip. But after two stinging cuts I think he became frightened. I must have looked like a black devil as I plunged and kicked, my eyes shining redly in the dusty gloom, my teeth snapping on empty air, as I could not snap them on him.

He got himself outside and banged the door to and I heard the thud of the crossbar drop into place. I felt trapped, but the commotion had routed the rats for the time being, which was a comfort. I was just beginning to simmer down and doze off when back they came, bolder than ever. Soon I was kicking away, so thoroughly roused now that even if the rats had gone I could not have slept a wink. Bang,

bang, bang! My hoofs echoed hollowly. Barsard stood it for about half an hour, and then he was back in a raging temper, but he did not come near me—only threatened me with sultry words for which I did not care a straw.

"You vicious brute! You wait till I get you out in the morning! I'll punish you!" he raved.

It was now open war between us, and I was determined that I would not submit to this man and his cruel treatment. I would soon show him that I had not been used to it and was far too proud and high-spirited to take it meekly. He did not come again, but I stamped and kicked till dawn, when the rats disappeared. How I longed for Andrea, who would have known in three seconds where the trouble lay. When the sunlight at last managed to penetrate some of the gloom of my ancient stables, and far away a cock's melody greeted the new day, I was done up.

I had thought I was tired last night, but I had been as fresh as spring larks compared to how I felt now. A quivery terror filled me that this would go on night after night— that I should never sleep again but die on my feet from complete exhaustion. I felt that I could eat no breakfast, but that was a small matter, for I was not given any for a long time. Besides other bad and lazy habits, Barsard was a late riser. His slovenly ways would not be tolerated for a moment where there was anyone who knew and understood animals. But in this place he was apparently his own master. He came slinking into the stables long past the proper time, and I wheeled and snorted, game even in my weariness. He gave me a look of hate, but he dared not openly neglect me, as he wanted the wage and could not afford to lose his position, though he was no doubt disgruntled that he had not a weak old hack to bully.

I was fed only a few moments before being saddled for Miss Nina to ride me out to her work, and I was not groomed

at all. The late feed could have been very dangerous—more
than one horse has been killed by exercise too soon after
eating, though your unhorsy man will have difficulty in be-
lieving it. But I had no appetite and turned away from my
corn in disgust.

When Miss Nina saw me she was horrified. "Oh, Rice,
he's sold me a wreck!" she cried. "I wouldn't have believed
that old Melville would have done that to me! I know—
I've read about it. They take ill-conditioned brutes with
failings that can be hidden for the time being so that they
give a flashy appearance and the poor buyer gets the thorny
end of the bargain. D'you think I ought to ride him? He
looks as if he'd drop apart. And Melville thought he would
be too spirited for me!"

"Spirited!" Barsard was beginning angrily, but he broke
off with a cough and glanced uneasily at his mistress. It
wasn't going to look well for him if I didn't thrive under
his care, or if my temper got bad and I bolted and threw
my Miss Nina and it could be proved that it was because of
his neglect and evil ways. "I think he'll be all right, lady,"
he finished hurriedly. "I should go easy at first, until he's
used to it!"

I was so pleased to get away from him and my awful
stable out into the April lanes that I actually began to perk
up a bit. It was queer having a lady on my back, and though
she was light enough I was expected to carry quite a lot of
her painting-gear too. But the warm sunshine was doing me
good in spite of the gnawing hunger which now began to
worry me. I was sorry I had been so offhand about my
breakfast.

Miss Nina sang little songs to herself as we went along.
The light had that bright hardness peculiar to spring; the
bunnies flicked across the fields, their tails winking at us
cheekily. A mistle-thrush called to us incessantly from a

tall aspen outside a big farm. When I saw a couple of big Suffolk punches being led out to work in the fields I longed to stop and speak to them. There had been a time when I should have despised myself for wanting to chat to common working-horses, so far beneath me in looks and breeding, as I thought, but I was desperate for companionship.

An ancient farmer with a face as wholesome as the soil he worked came to the lane gate as we went by.

"Why, eff it ain't Miss Marsh back!" he exclaimed. "Now that be spring for sure, mate, now that she be back at her painting. And I hear ye've taken the cottage fer this year?" He smacked his hand down on the gate bar as if he were as pleased as a king about it all. Then his glance rested on me. "Hello, Miss Marsh, and what hev we here?" he went on dubiously. "I did say, last year, that by the good rights ye should ride and not walk, but what's this ye're on? Something a bit wrong there that wants altering. Don't, and ye'll be sorry."

"I know; that's why I came past here; I wanted to ask you," my rider said, and I could feel her soft, warm little hand on my neck, and I knew the look of the worried little frown that must be creasing her brows as she explained how she had loved my fine looks at the circus a month ago and could hardly recognise me now.

"Has he been frightened?" Farmer Graves asked suspiciously.

"Why, no; not that I know of," Miss Nina replied slowly. Graves felt me all over and I knew by his touch that he could read horses as a man reads print. He found a little sore place where I had hurt myself kicking last night.

"That pond been drained lately?" he asked.

"What's that got to do with it?"

"Everything," Graves answered quietly. He came and stood by my head and fondled me. "Poor fellow, poor old fellow! You've been through it proper. That was no break-fast, being as how you were too upset to eat. No one to clean your coat properly. Look, Miss Marsh. Ye've got a beauty here and he's well worth looking after. Now, will ye take an old man's advice, eh?"

"Of course I will. I told you that was why I came. Until my brother gets here I've no one to help me."

"Why, then, you go and make a doddy wee picture of them little old buttercups down in the water-meadow where ye were working last year, and I'll give this chap something to be going along with. Then, if ye'll give permission, I'll send Jake an' Allen to open up that old dyke and drain yer pond. It's rats what's at the bottom of this little old spot of trouble; that it is!"

After bad times good times are lovely. I had no fear of going with the good farmer and he had no fear of me. How delicious was that feed he gave me and the careful grooming that I got from quick, skilful hands. I felt that I should never be bad-tempered again, and I sidled and pranced a little, though I was too sleepy to be very uppish. But my greatest surprise and pleasure was yet to come, for on this day of my life began a friendship which lasted many months. I am not talking of my liking for Miss Marsh or Farmer Graves, for I knew them for less than a year, but of my chumship with Flopsy, the greatest little comrade any horse could have.

CHAPTER THIRTEEN

THE COMING OF FLOPSY

I DID not meet her till that evening. Miss Nina had brought her lunch with her, so, when Graves had done with me, he let me out into the buttercup-field without saddle or bridle on for a little rest.

I could not have believed that it would feel so wonderful to be absolutely free again. I galloped and kicked and rolled on the lush grass. Not since I had been a colt had I felt anything so pleasant. My mistress laughed to see me and then she began making sketches of me, but I would not stay still for that.

I could see that there was an extremely thoughtful look on her face once or twice, for the care and grooming and, more than that, the consideration I had received from the farmer, had done great things for me and I must have looked much more like the flashing black perfection she had seen at the circus. I felt that she was beginning to blame Barsard in her mind, and I was not sorry in the least.

That was a glorious day. When the sun got hotter later in the afternoon I stood under the alders and willows and dozed pleasantly, while a little stream chuckled and lisped to itself over the stones near by. But at last the sun began to go down and Farmer Graves came to catch me. Would I let him? Not at first! But I felt no anger when, by a clever trick, he caught me and saddled me up for Miss Nina. Fair treatment would always secure fair service from me. I know that there are many noble-hearted beasts who will work and toil willingly for brutes who ought to be saddled and bridled themselves, and who will take their hard lot uncomplain-ingly. But I was certainly not one of them.

"Now, Miss Marsh," the farmer said, "my men have set that pond to drain. It won't do away wi' all them little old rats, but it'll go a long way. And they've taken Flopsy over to your place. She's yours now, ma'am, and I reckon Stardust here will be the better for her help and company. Eh, old man?" he asked and slapped me jokingly. I shook my mane proudly and flicked my magnificent tail from side to side. Graves watched me admiringly.

"You be careful, Miss Nina, that he ain't pinched," he said. "You've a very valuable horse there!"

As we neared home some of my happy delight began to ooze from me. The very memory of Barsard's thin, squeezed face and mean needle-eyes began to depress me, so that I felt my ears flatten instinctively. He came forward as soon as we rode up to the cottage, and reached for my reins. I snapped warningly at him and he scowled darkly, but did nothing worse. I allowed myself to be led into my stall, and, to my surprise, found it thick with good, clean straw. A long day to himself in which to do some hard thinking had, no doubt, done Barsard a lot of good. He made no attempt to clout or cuff me, so I let him see to me and I enjoyed the supper he brought me.

And then I had my great surprise. Miss Nina came from the cottage, and she was carrying a large hamper.

"Here's your stable-companion," she said in the light, happy tones which even today, over twenty-three years after, I remember so well. She flung back the lid, and there sat an enormous young dark-sand-coloured cat with topaz eyes and the most immense whiskers I ever saw on any cat.

"Flopsy, here is Stardust. You're going to help him and be friends." She turned to the groom. "It's all right, Rice; Flopsy is used to horses. Farmer Graves said so!"

"But look at *him*!" Barsard pointed, and I fancied there was triumphant contempt in his voice. At the first sight and smell of cat I seemed to freeze with horror, though I am bound to confess that my good horse-sense told me that this was a very different kind of cat from the one that had made such a disastrous break in my life. But it was still cat and all at once all my old strung-up temper flared at the thought of its coming near me or touching me. *That* idea I just could not bear. With teeth flashing, I lunged at it, and the cat said "Spsssst!" and leapt for the partition and from there to the hay, where she crouched in the opening, staring down, her topaz moons full of that detached look of disdain which is so much a part of all cats.

"Oh, dear!" said Miss Nina. "Oh, dear me, he'll kill it! And I was so sure it would help."

"You needn't fear for that old mouser!" Barsard spat, and wiped his mouth on the back of his hand. "She's used to looking after herself; you can see that. Shut the door, if you please, after the two of us. My hands are full."

Though she looked a little amazed and annoyed at the man's cheek, Miss Nina did as she was bid and they went out. No doubt she thought it was for the best, but I was keyed up and in a blaze of quite evil temper. It was bad enough to have a cat anywhere about, but to have it near me in the dark—that was the last straw!

I kicked out once or twice just for the satisfaction of hearing my hoofs smash splinteringly on the crazy woodwork already dented by last night's performance. There was no Andrea to soothe and understand me, no bright life and glitter about me as in the circus days to distract my thoughts.

Then, suddenly, I had to stop and listen in a cold sweat of fear, listen to find out if it was moving about or coming any nearer. I had worked myself into a proper lather of excitement and now as I stood there with my sides heaving

I couldn't hear a thing but the plunk-plunk of water dripping from the stable-tap into a trough. And then my heart sank, for I did hear something and it was not the cat—it was the old scurrying of the rats just as during last night, though there did not seem to be nearly so many. A shaft of moonlight had worked round to where it fell like a silver bar into one corner of my stall and so tonight I could see the wretched vermin better as they loped and undulated on their way.

But I saw also two bright eyes shining redly, floating along near the floor. Next second there was a warm flurry of fur, a tail whisked against my feet, and there was a squeal from the cornered rat which ended in a worrying, thumping little whirlwind of sound, to be succeeded by silence as if all the other rats had paused affrighted at what had happened to their comrade.

Flopsy was sitting up quietly and licking her shoulder fur, rumpled by the rat's teeth. She did not look at me. She did not seem to care if I were watching or no. I realised that this was a game to her, the most thrilling of sport, and I knew now why Farmer Graves had sent her over. I felt ashamed of the way I had greeted her, for now she was away after another rat and this time the battle raged on up to a crossbeam and down a wall, for it was an old buck-rat determined to make a great bid for life. But he did not know what I learned later—that Flopsy was famed throughout the county as a ratter.

Flopsy killed her rat over against the door and then came pacing sedately back, shaking one paw daintily. She looked as if she thought the place sadly neglected and that there was a lot of work for her to do. I felt rather small for the way I had behaved and I told her so, but I doubt if she heard or understood me. But her presence was now the most comforting thing I had ever imagined. Here was a real friend, someone who hated those awful rats as much as I did. Before I knew where I was I had actually dropped off to sleep in my warm straw and had the finest night's rest I ever remember.

I woke so refreshed and comforted that life had taken on again some of that golden glitter of happiness I used to know. What a sight I saw! Flopsy had had a wonderful time, to judge by results. There were dead rats everywhere. Their stiff grey bodies lay twisted this way and that. One hung grotesquely, caught by its haunches between the bars of a hay rack. I wondered where the cat was, for nowhere could I hear her moving about. Then something made me look down and there she was curled up comfortably in the corner of my own stall. She was so much the colour of the straw that at first I had not noticed. Her eyes were tight shut, her whiskered jaws were curved in the cat grin which never leaves these animals even when asleep. Now and again a paw twitched as if she were dreaming. I hardly dared move now; I was so afraid of treading on her and hurting her. I told you that all my life if anything shows complete trust in me I react at once. Mind you, it had to be the real thing, not just a show of bravery to cover a hidden terror of me—though this last was courage too and always won my respect; just to know that someone feared me and was trying not to let me know made me jumpy myself and then neither could help the other.

Flopsy merely seemed to take it for granted that she was safe, and so she was from me. When Barsard came—late, of course—to feed me she awoke, slipped past his blundering feet, and was away to the cottage for her saucer of bread-and-milk.

The man was quieter, and I could not help thinking that Miss Nina had been giving him a piece of her mind. But there was a subdued glitter of dislike in his eyes and I knew he hated me and would try and get even if he could without being detected.

CHAPTER FOURTEEN

MORE TROUBLE FOR ME

THERE was quite an air of anticipation about Miss Nina that morning, and I found she was not going painting. Instead, she rode me to the station to meet her brother. I was more than a bit disappointed, for the memory of that lazy day among the buttercups was still fresh in my mind. But I liked my rider and I wanted so much to please her. So, when she was mounted, I carried her as carefully as if she had been made of glass.

Halfway there, however, she patted my shoulder and said, laughingly: "Come, come, Stardust; I feel sure you can do better than this!"

She put me into a gallop, and we had a magnificent burst, which did my heart good, though I am bound to confess that I felt a bit puffy owing to having had such a late breakfast.

When the train arrived and Haldane Marsh got out I was very pleased with him. He was tall and broad and brown, as if he had just come from a country of sunshine. As a matter of fact, he had, for I heard later that he held a Government job in Egypt. He could not get over his delight in me, but walked all round me, felt me all over, patted me, and generally made much of me.

"Never thought a sister of mine could pick a horse," he teased her. "He's like a horse in a picture. I say, what lovely country too! There's no place like England. So this is where you came last year while I was toiling and sweating at Alagra, building that dam!"

She wanted him to ride me, but he walked beside us and she pointed out all the beauty-spots that she hoped to paint that year. We passed one place that I had noted before, but now I heard all about it. A wire lattice-fence enclosed some seventy acres of wonderful parkland, with heavy woods, lush meadows, rolling grassland and heathy tracts, all watered by a broad silver stream on the banks of which the wild forget-me-nots stared up with happy eyes at a sky as blue as they were. All this place, she told Haldane, belonged to an old recluse called Silas Weatherbeam, who had made the estate a sanctuary for wild life.

"He's thrilled too with all animals," Miss Nina went on: "horses and dogs and cats, and he keeps buying them up to save them from a miserable old age."

"Stout fellow!" The man laughed. "Must have a heavy feed bill at his place."

"Yes, I should imagine so, but he's awfully rich. They say there are seventy old horses and as many dogs and cats. Sometimes you can see——"

She reined me in and pointed. I looked with great interest, for I had never heard of anything like this before. It was true. About twenty horses, fine old hunters, two down-at-heel dray horses and some old cabby's wrecks, were moving about the field just below us, revelling peacefully in the sunshine and the sweet grass. Their steel shoes, symbol of service, had been removed for the last time in their lives and no work would ever again be required of them. As we watched, a pack of joyous dogs led a stampede of ponies down to the stream, where the dogs rolled and played and splashed to their hearts' content.

I thought then how awful it must be to get old and be at the mercy of hard owners who did not agree with Silas Weatherbeam, whom men called a soft-headed old fool. They were the soft-heads themselves who said it.

We got back to the cottage and they went in to lunch. Barsard had groomed me after a fashion that morning, but it was not the thorough business to which I had been used. He had the wicked habit some grooms indulge in of occasionally running the curry-comb over *me,* instead of using it for its real purpose. The sharp prongs hurt me and made me prance skittishly, and Barsard laughed to see it. Many a good horse has been turned into a brute by this one bit of cruelty alone.

Then, in sullen silence, he brought me my food. While I was eating, Flopsy came in with quite an air of importance, stalked straight into my stall, and began treading out her corner in my newly shaken-up bedding. I longed to tell her how happy she had made me, but did not know how, so I reached down my long neck and touched her golden back with my nose. Immediately she arched herself against me, pressing hard and leaning sideways in the quaint delight a cat shows when being rubbed. A fine, deep, crooning purr woke in her throat till she roared like a small railway-engine. We were now firm friends and I was very happy.

The next few days were very pleasant, and if only my groom had been another Andrea life would have been perfect. It never is, I believe, but it was pretty good, all the same. Every night there were fewer rats and Flopsy was in great form. I was soon at the stage when I hardly knew how I had ever got on without her. I did not mind now if she moved about around my feet in the darkness; I loved, indeed, to feel the soft warmth of her furry coat as she rubbed against my legs in greeting.

I thought next morning that Haldane looked at me in some doubt when I was led out. Miss Nina was doing a painting of the cottage itself, so my new master said he would exercise me. A little husk from my breakfast had blown into my mane and he picked it out and stood looking at it, turning it over and over in his fingers, crushing it together with little crispy sounds.

"Barsard, when did you feed this horse?"

A shifty look of detected ill-doing flashed for a moment in the needle-like eyes. Then the groom's face was a mask again.

"Two hours ago, sir," he lied glibly.

I sensed that my master was not satisfied, but he said nothing more, only mounted me and rode off. We had a wonderful ride, but he did not press me at all, so I was not distressed. He was a determined sort of person, however, who once he had made up his mind about a thing would let nothing stop him from what he considered to be his duty.

Long after all was quiet that night the stable-door wheezed softly on its hinges, letting in the scented, moonlit air. Haldane, carrying a rug, stepped quietly in and closed the door behind him. He spoke to me so that I should recognise his voice and not be nervous, and I was grateful.

There was a great deal of rustling and swishing in the straw in a clean empty stall; he grunted as he settled down for the night. Flopsy raised her head from her washing operations and mewed her opinion of the interruption, but soon all was as peaceful as before.

I must say that I was tremendously curious about it all, and I reflected how queer all man-animals were. Fancy sleeping here on the straw near me when he had his own place at the cottage! I had difficulty in getting off to sleep for thinking of it, and moved impatiently about for a time. If he noticed, he never grumbled or swore at me, but lay still on his rug. He was up at six, even before Flopsy had finished her morning washing.

"Come on; clear out, old lady," he said pleasantly to her and bundled her gently out of her corner, so that she "fuffed" at him and fled up on the beams out of the way.

Haldane began by cleaning and filling my water-bucket and giving me some sweet hay to keep me amused while he cleaned out the soiled straw and generally tidied up. Then, about seven, he brought me my breakfast. It was lovely having it so good and early, as in the old days. He patted me and admired me, then went on tidying up, leaving me to get on with my food.

About a quarter past nine the door opened and Barsard came in, hurrying furtively as he always did, as if by putting on a show of speed he could persuade casual onlookers that he was well-meaning but had been unavoidably detained. Haldane was at the far end of the small building, but because of the tiny windows and poor lighting he could not be seen if he kept still. He kept still and then I began to see his game. He was going to find out for himself just how late and careless was this man whom Miss Nina had hired and about whom he, Haldane, had grave suspicions.

"Now then, you brute," the groom muttered to me, "I'll get your oats or else that man will say something!"

I showed the whites of my eyes and laid back my ears at the very sound of Barsard's voice; I could not help it. He went, grumbling and spitting, across to the oats-bin, but he never got me the food I did not need. Haldane came out of his dark corner and his face was very angry. He could look blacker than any man I ever knew.

"Don't exert yourself, Barsard," he began sarcastically. "I have fed Stardust. Is this an hour to begin work? If I'd had you among my men in Egypt I'd have licked you into better shape than this in the first hour, you selfish cur!"

"I'm sorry, sir," Rice Barsard began to whine, for he was a coward as well as a bully, and Haldane frightened him. Haldane frightened *me* with that look on his face. "I did sleep a little late this morning, sir, but it hasn't never happened before and it shan't occur again."

"It has happened before," Haldane said stonily. "Don't think to get out of it like that. But it shan't happen again

—not here, at any rate. Get out of my stables and don't ever let me see your mean face again or I may forget myself and knock you down!"

"Here, you can't dismiss me like that," Barsard began to bluster. "This is a good place, and Miss Marsh she was quite suited; and, anyway, it was her what employed me and not you, sir!"

"We will leave my sister's name out of this," Haldane stated coldly. "Now, get out, do you hear?"

Fury blazed up in my master's eyes and he took a step forward as he spoke. The groom scuttled out into the yard. Here he turned raving and cringing like a sick dog.

"All right, sir," he snarled with a string of oaths. "I'll get even someday. I'll have my revenge if it's the last thing I do!"

"Get *out*!" Haldane roared, and he picked up an iron bar used for propping open the cornbin. Barsard fled to his hut, from whence he emerged in five minutes carrying an old leather case with his belongings. I believe that Miss Nina paid him something, because he had no notice, but I don't think he deserved a copper farthing. The very air seemed cleaner and sweeter when he had gone and I wished that he would never cross my path again.

CHAPTER FIFTEEN

TIME BRINGS CHANGES

FOR the rest of Haldane's leave he groomed me himself, fed me and looked after me, and I had no complaints. Flopsy and I were as close as two chums can be, and she trusted me in a way that made me very proud and happy.

The spring that year had been very heavenly and now it gave way to a peerless summer. The lanes were pink with the sweet faces of the dogroses, the yellow-hammers twittered and drew out their long, lazy, song notes that were a very symbol of hot high summertide.

Miss Nina was gay as a robin as she painted a wonderful picture of me, which, to this day, I believe, hangs in some famous gallery in London. Then came the sad day towards the end of July when my master's leave was running out; packings and portmanteaux were the order of the day.

She cried a lot when we were alone together, but she was very gay and carefree in front of her brother. I think he suspected as much, but he also seemed to take great care to be natural and light-hearted. Like two children who have broken a favourite toy and are miserable without it, they pretended very hard that they didn't care.

But time ticked away. At last the train bore Haldane Marsh away, and Miss Nina did not go out painting for two whole days. As he knew that I should need attention when he was gone he had arranged for a new groom, had interviewed him himself, and felt fairly happy about his choice, for I heard him tell his sister on the last day that Patrick was a good, kind lad who would not tread on a worm if he could help it.

Patrick came next day, a fresh-faced country boy with sleepy eyes and freckles so thick that they ran together in brown patches like autumn-leaves. He had been taught to groom a horse and look after it and was very careful, almost too careful, for he was slow. Still, that was a fault on the right side and he was hardworking. But because he had not yet spent years of working with horses, it was perhaps asking rather a lot of him to make him solely responsible, for, when he forgot anything, there was no one over him to check and remind him. Sometimes he forgot to groom me and twice he forgot to put on my night rug. It did not greatly matter in those wonderful August nights, but still, it was a fault.

One day I remembered well, for it might have had a terrible end. Flopsy was very restless and kept wandering about the stable mewing and pushing her nose into all sorts of places that ordinarily she would never have noticed. Finally, she settled at my feet in her old corner. I had finished my hay and thought to have a cool drink, for the morning was unusually sultry, with a weight in it of coming thunder. A drowsy expectancy hung over everything, and even the swallows under the eaves chittered in a subdued way.

I reached down for a drink in my nice, clean bucket, only to see with a shock that it was not there. When one is used to a certain thing in a certain place one never thinks twice about it until it is missing and then the blank is like a blow in the face. I lipped at the partition in an aimless sort of way, wondering what on earth I was to do. My thirst, which had been real enough before, was now maddening, just because I knew I could not slake it. I heard Patrick's footsteps in the yard and thought he must have remembered and be hurrying back to put matters right. But he went on with some work he was doing and I stamped and pawed impatiently until Flopsy turned up large reproachful eyes at me. Then I noticed that she had given birth to three of the fattest kittens you ever saw and she was busy combing and cleaning them in perfect faith that her big friend would not hurt them.

In my delight, I forgot for a time the agony of my growing thirst. Shrill little sounds like gnats playing on reeds came from those three-inch cushions with their rounded heads and gummed-up eyes. Tired but happy, Flopsy lay back as the kittens fed, her eyes closed in content, a smile curving her furry jaws. Perhaps when Miss Nina came to look at the kittens she would notice my plight and get me a drink. I heard her voice as she called to the groom.

"Patrick, oh, Pat! It looks so bad I don't think I'll go out today. Give Stardust his exercise as usual."

A door banged gently and she had gone back into the cottage. Patrick came to me, saddled me up and led me out, but he never noticed about the bucket. His face lit up, though, when he saw Flopsy's kindle of kittens, for in spite of his lack of thought he was genuinely fond of animals. Even the best of intentions, however, cannot make up for carelessness like his. We did not go too far, but the heat was terrible. It was that kind of hot damp heat that makes everything limp as a wilting weed. I felt dizzy and my tongue seemed to be too big for me. Twice I stumbled.

"Hold up," Patrick chirruped to me cheerfully, but I did not feel cheerful.

When we got back my mouth was sore, and foam was dashed in long white flakes on my black coat. The boy took me in and pottered about in his slow, careful way. Oh, how I longed to hear the chink of the iron bucket, but it did not come and the afternoon grew hotter still. The sun had gone behind low-hung black clouds and in the distance swelled a continual muttering of coming trouble. I pulled at my fastenings and stamped restlessly, then remembered the kittens and stood still, my head down, my eyes fixed in dull misery on the floor.

The colour of the straw whitened, and darkened again as a vivid flash whipped across the leaden sky outside. There was a hot pause and then the thunder banged and rolled past, dying to a mutter. With a swish, the rain hit us and soon the chuckle of water foaming into the tub under the eaves grew to a roar. An occasional drop even found its way through the roof and fell like a silver pea in the gloom.

I think it was worse to be so thirsty and hear the wet gurgle of so much water and not be able to reach it. I began to moan in my misery; my tongue was hanging out and my sides heaved as I sighed. Running steps came across the yard and Miss Nina and the boy came in.

"There, miss," he was saying in delight. "See, there, by Stardust's feet. Ain't they lovely?"

"They certainly are," said the sweet voice, and Miss Nina bent to look at them. "Come, they will be wet and cold here. Come, Flopsy, we'll take you all across to the house out of this storm!"

Flopsy mewed her protest, but she and her little family were gently but firmly carried out, sheltered with some old sacking. The stable door swung to, its catch-hook rattling, and I was alone.

There was nothing now to take my unhappy thoughts off myself, and I began to realise how very fond I had grown of the yellow farm-cat. The rain went on drumming and splashing and the already gloomy afternoon darkened to a wet evening. The storm had apparently made Patrick forget my afternoon feed, but it did not matter. I was far too dry to have swallowed a single oat.

It was Flopsy who saved me at last, though she did not

know it! The door to the stable, unfastened, kept gathering itself up in small eddies of wind and opening as if it were alive and had decided to move about and see the world. Then the eddy would die and it would return to its place with a squealing thud. The monotonous sound almost drove me crazy. It was so dark now that I could see little, so I was startled to see a shadow creep in during one of the door's erratic swings, and slip quietly across to the old corner. It was Flopsy and she was carrying a fat kitten.

She tucked it firmly into the straw, glanced up as if to say: "Keep an eye on it," and then whirled out again. I was greatly thrilled at her trust and put down my head to sniff the kitten, but I blew the straw about and seemed to upset it, so waited patiently to see what would happen next. Back fussed Flopsy with another kitten, and then the third. She knew what was best for her family, and no human was going to interfere if she could help it! Hard on her heels came Miss Nina and Patrick with a lantern. She was laughing, happy-eyed, and more like her old self.

"Oh, the poor dear darling! Of course she shall be here if she likes it best," she said. "Patrick, get them some water and I'll send their supper over. Stay, you can fill that little dish from Stardust's bucket!"

There was a startled pause, and then, in quite a different tone, she exclaimed sharply: "Patrick! Where's the horse's bucket?"

"It's there, miss, ain't it?" came the lad's cheerful rejoinder.

"No, it *isn't*! And, oh, look at Stardust! How long has he been without?"

"Oh, miss, I don't know; I'm so sorry, miss. I could have sworn I filled it this morning."

Miss Nina was too shocked to protest, but dashed off and with her own hands fetched my pail and filled it. She brought it and I struggled to get at it almost before she had time to put it down, so that some was spilled over her dress. She did not care about that, but she turned and in a quiet but firm way gave Patrick the most useful dressing-down I ever heard a lad receive. It was good for him. One such mistake and one such lecture would not easily be forgotten and a habit of easy-going carelessness which might have grown to a grave fault had been checked. But from what I heard after I gathered that this happening decided her not to do as she had intended and keep me in town over the winter. Without her brother to help and advise she felt she knew too little about such matters to risk any more mistakes. Patrick sobbed and sobbed and the rain continued to tumble down as if the very skies were weeping too.

As for me, no drink I ever had before or since was so sweet as that bucketful of tepid water. I sucked and sucked, and I would have liked a lot more, but Miss Nina would not give me too much all at once, not quite sure whether or no it would be wise. She returned later in the evening and stood over the boy to see I had all I needed. When she went she looked unhappy and troubled.

So that settled it. By the time Flopsy's kittens were eight weeks old and ready to leave for their new homes at various farms, it was time for Miss Nina to return to town. The little household in the honeysuckle cottage prepared to pack up and disband. An advertisement was put in several big papers about me and a number of people came to see me. But I don't like strangers pawing me over, so as soon as anyone came near I flattened my ears and swished my tail just to let them know how I felt.

"Lot of vice in that beast," one man said nervously and backed off.

But there was no vice in me *then*, only an independent temper. But those people were sure I was a biter and a kicker and no one bid for me. Miss Nina began to get worried. Autumn was on us and winter coming along fast, for it was already into October. She was due back in town on some winter commissions. The red-and-gold leaves of the maples were scurrying down off the trees and heaping themselves in corners to lie crisp and rustling. Mice crept into outhouses to feed fat on stored grain. Overhead, long lines of geese drove south, sending down their haunting trumpet-calls to stir the blood with I don't know what half-understood longings. Flopsy and I were now such pals that I would go nowhere and do nothing without her. Patrick remarked as much one day.

"If you sells Stardust, Miss Marsh, you'll have to let the old cat go too, I reckon, or he'll not stir a hoof out of the place!"

"I think you're right," she answered, looking dubiously at me, for she had grown very fond of me and was sorry to lose me, I knew.

One day she brought a little, fussy, fat man to see me. He used his hands as much as his mouth when talking and his English was broken and uneven, but he fell for me and almost capered in his delight.

"Ah, mademoiselle," he cried, "all my life have I wanted to possess a so proud, a so beautiful horse. He is of ze legends, yes. He is ze very horse of ze poem of ze Arab's farewell, yes?"

He skipped up to me and somehow I did not mind him but turned mildly to look at him.

"So beautiful, so kind," he said and then bent down to stroke Flopsy, who was leaning on his legs and rubbing her sides and purring. "She is like my own minou-chat, my well-beloved one! And she is ze friend of ze Stardust, you say? Good. I take her too, yes, no?"

I was pleased to see the queer little fellow stroking my

chum and tickling her furry ears, and I nickered softly. The
Frenchman clapped his hands and Miss Nina laughed.

"They seem to have settled that, Mr. Dubois," she said.
"Have you bought any other horses over here?"

"Two only." Paul Dubois nodded his head vigorously. "I
take them back with me to my own home, yes, no? I do
not go on ze same boat, but I will send for ze horse next
week. He goes from Harwich."

He departed in a perfect whirlwind of waving fingers, and
Flopsy came to rub herself against me for a change. I felt
pleased that my life was to change again and that I was to see
new places. Who knew but I might meet Andrea again?
Somewhere deep down inside me was the hope that I might
once more hear his voice. The hope was slowly dying as the
weeks drew out into months, but it was yet there.

On the Wednesday morning, Patrick gave me a last
grooming, and Flopsy was shut up into a roomy hamper, at
which indignity she protested loudly. The lad had been very
subdued since that mistake about the water. Now the tears
stood in his eyes and his freckled face was red with emotion,
which gave him a mottled look that was very comical.

Miss Nina said goodbye regretfully, and then they came
with a special horse-box for me, drawn by a sturdy old
work-horse. The cat's hamper was placed in with me, as I
showed plainly that I was going to act ugly unless I had my
pal.

So I left Honeysuckle Cottage, and I have never seen it
since. Who lives there now, I wonder? Do other horses
stand in those old-world, stuffy stables and kick the rotten
partition because of the rats?

My journey was by road this time and I liked it far better
than the train. Also, I was better looked after. I did not miss
a single meal and it was all very pleasant. At one stopping-
place, I thought I saw, far off in the distance, some caravans

in a field and I was very excited, but of course I could not explain that I wanted to gallop off to see them.

We reached Harwich after dark. It was a gloomy evening and a light, cold drizzle was being blown along by a heavy gale; the roads gleamed like glass below the shining street lamps. The shadows and the dazzle made it difficult to see where the quay ended and the water began, but I knew! We horses have sixth senses where such things are concerned, but they told the driver of my horse-box that, only the week before, a truck which was being man-handled into position had gone over the edge, taking the men with it.

The boat was to sail with the tide at ten-thirty, so it was high time I was on board. Some porters came to take over and one of them lifted Flopsy's hamper on to his shoulders. The outline of the vessel was an inky mass pierced with round patterns of golden light. A big loading-light overhead gleamed on the broad goods gangway with its crossbars. This gangway led to the deck, where was a shelter with stalls in it—a permanency, for this boat often carried horses to the Continent.

"Can't put this here hamper in with the hosses," one porter said. "They be too narrow, them stalls, as it is!"

This was dreadful news to me and I wished that my new owner was on the boat, as he would have seen to it. I reared up my head to look after the hamper and I began to whinny shrilly and stamp with my feet.

"Here, look at that!" One of the men backed off in fear, for in that light I must have loomed much bigger than I was, a monster horse, the light rippling on the black satin of my coat, my nostrils blood-red as they widened with my warning snorts.

"That's right," the other man shouted. "The quay boss said to look out. He'd heard reports of this brute. For goodness' sake bring that 'amper over here or he'll kick a hole in the steamer."

"But it's too big," his companion wailed, and at that moment Flopsy, no doubt terrified, added her voice. Her strident mews were woeful to hear and I lost my head and reared in my anxiety for her.

"Open it, George! The cat will have to go loose with him in his stall, and if there's trouble we can't help it," the first man whispered. "Quick, before the boss sees us! If the cat makes off, they can't blame us, and what's a cat more or less?"

So Flopsy's hamper was undone and I quieted down. As things turned out it was the saving of my pal's life, as if she had remained shut in she would have been drowned. So, in a way, I had been able to repay her something of all that she had done for me.

The stalls were certainly very narrow, but the cat curled up at my feet, crooning her relief at being out of her cramping quarters. There were three other horses besides myself. When the men had tied us up securely they went out and banged and bolted the doors, so that we felt dreadfully trapped.

But it was a tremendous pleasure to me to be near some of my own kind again and I became very friendly at once with them, or at least with the two of them who were each side of me. The other horse, Rupert, I never knew so well. But Bran and Alex were magnificent beasts, hunters and thoroughbreds. They asked questions about me and told me bits of their lives and I was cheered and happy in a way I could not have believed a while ago. I showed them Flopsy, and they were politely interested, but seemed to think I had been hard pressed to make friends with a cat.

A turmoil of sound was going on outside: the slow whistle of ropes over the sheaves of blocks where the deck-cranes were working, the banging and shunting from the nearby goods-trains, shouts, and the hoots of sirens. Added to which the wind was increasing and was now moaning overhead in the rigging, thumbing long-drawn-out notes on the funnel-stays. Below us in the heart of the vessel a wallowing thump began to vibrate itself through to every inch of deck and walls. It was as bad as the train—it was even worse, for though the train rocked this thing we were on rolled slowly and ponderously from side to side in a way that made our stomachs feel sick and empty.

We were steaming away steadily now into the inky night, but all round us were other vessels coming and going. We could hear the swish of green seas at their cutwaters and an occasional blare and blurt of warning. The other horses were as terrified as I was, and as cold and sick. Flopsy cuddled against my feet and mewed piteously. Had we two known that the wildest part of our adventurous lives was only just ahead of us, when for many months we should own no man master, we should have been even more alarmed than we were.

How far away already seemed the firm ground, the sunny lanes and English fields, the summer song of larks, and the breath of the long-past faded dog-roses! The wild salt tang of the North Sea was all about us.

With a crackle and splash, the waves were beginning to break over the bows and wash along the iron decks. Thin sheets of water with wide half-moons of foam crusting their edges slid under the partition walls and slid out again, carrying long straws with them. As the roll increased, I found that I could not help staggering slightly and I was dreadfully afraid of hurting Flopsy, but she was too sick to care.

Once a man came in hurriedly with a lantern to see if we were all right. He could scarcely hold the door from being blown off its hinges and he looked wild and bedraggled in spite of black oilskins and sou'wester.

"They're all right, Bill," we heard him scream against the gale and he fought the door shut.

I was thankful, for if it had seemed noisy and cold in our prison before it now appeared snug and quiet compared to the storm racket out on deck.

Endlessly the hours dragged and we forged slowly ahead into the stiffest gale known on that coast for many years.

CHAPTER SIXTEEN

I RUN WILD

Ours was not the only wreck that night. Up and down the
Channel, on the French coast, on the flats of Holland, and
on the grim North Sea itself, gallant vessels drove to their
deaths. Broken bones of them stared gauntly at the morrow's
sun when it came at last to chase away the purple shadows
of the storm. Cattle-boats and clippers, steamers and mail-
packets, all went the same way; they were pitilessly torn and
washed apart to spill their cargoes on lonely sandbanks, and
drown the men who had ventured out in them.

Our hour came in the first grey light of that late autumn
morning. We went aground on the Essex sandbanks, blown
far off our course. I felt the soft shock as she ran her nose
into the clinging mud which was to hold her so that, drop-
ping with the tide, she broke her back and opened up like a
rotten fish-basket.

A clamour of terror broke out. Feet stamped as men ran;
gear, slatting uselessly, banged and stormed aloft. The
dreary, drawn-out blasts on the steamer's siren, calling
vainly for aid where no aid could come, echoed into the
driving rain.

With the uncanny knowledge that catastrophe was upon
us, we set up a stamping and rattling in our fear, snorting and
nickering. They came to get us out, of course. No man worth
his salt will abandon his dumb friends without an effort;
only, unfortunately, man cannot hide from his inner feelings. Many a proud huntsman or circus trick-rider would
be humiliated and perhaps made so fearful that he dared not
ride if he could guess that his every emotion is known to us:

all his carefully hidden fears of the dangerous jump or neck-risking gallop sensed by us just as he feels them.

So, when two seamen came and flung open the doors and stormed in on us, driven as it were on a wall of freezing water, for the decks were awash, we knew that even more than the gale they were afraid of us. They had had nothing to do with horses on boats, having only recently joined our vessel, and to them we were maddened demons who would turn on them if loosed. But for all that, they did not shrink from their duty.

"Come, lend a hand, Bill, and unship the brutes; then they'll have to shift for themselves," one cried.

Would we follow them? Of course we would not. Fire and flood and storm do funny things to horses. I suppose we feel more secure if we stay where, if only for a time, the surroundings have become familiar to us. It is foolish, I know, but we have not the imagination of man and we cannot always see where the thing will end.

So we resisted, backed and struggled, shrieked and tried to bite in our terror. There came a warning shout from the deck. The boats were being manned. They were abandoning us to die out here in the foam and smother of the breaking-up. But still we would not have gone with them. They ran down the clanging deck; there were shouts and orders and then a roar as they launched the boats.

And then we heard no more the voices of men. We were alone. I don't know how long it was, counting as men count time, before the old vessel was finally washed apart. Seas broke and slammed over us; a deep shuddering, which began as a faint tremble in the hull, grew and grew till at each wave we could hear crackings and boomings as the strained fabric parted.

I was knee-deep in water soon, and poor Flopsy, trembling with cold, leaped up on the partition, where she stood mewing desperately. Her fur was soaked with salt water so that it stood out in spikes and she shook and shook her frozen paws. Perhaps she thought my fine broad back was warmer and pleasanter to her feet, for she took a little jump with cold-stiffened paws, thumped a small mew out of herself as she landed, and then settled in a cat-crouch, forepaws drawn under her chest.

Alex, the brown hunter on my right, nodded his head up and down as if to ease tired muscles.

"That cat's got sense," he said shortly. "She knows enough to keep in with something that swims!"

I thought of all the cold salt miles we must have come. To me it seemed as if the shore must be hundreds of miles away and I said so.

"Swim?" I cried incredulously. "We are only horses, after all!"

Bran lipped at his own leg as if wondering whether anything that felt so woodenly frozen could still be used. "I must say that it seems fantastic to me," he said.

But Alex shook himself. "You believe me. Swim for all you're worth, if this—" he stamped at the deck—"if this lets us down. The way they were heading was round the coastline. I have been over before, so I know. Though you have been sailing for hours you are still only a short way from your home-beaches. As we are unfastened we may, with skill and a little luck, yet eat tomorrow's corn!"

After that there was little more talk, for the storm-cry was so deafening that we just stood and shuddered to hear it. There was a great cracking overhead, a wallowing lurch, and the roofing over us parted to show the racing dawn-clouds blotting out and uncovering the paling stars, so that it seemed as if the whole heavens were swinging. The rain had almost stopped, leaving only the razor-breath of the wind.

Another crack and the partition walls of our shelter melted

in the half light as if they had never been, and we were upon the foundering deck. I stared out to see what the world looked like now and it was indeed a grim picture of green desolation. We were almost level with the long endless lines of waves shouldering in over the treacherous sands. The flash and splinter of their impact on the vessel, now a log-like, inert obstruction in their path, filled the air with water-jewels.

At each stunning blow the poor old vessel heeled and heeled a little more, groaning as she broke apart. The decks sloped below us now, so that we could not keep our footing but slipped and struggled to where the rail had been. One more lurch and we were in the sea and swimming desperately for our lives. Our heads were held high as with terror-filled eyes we gazed ahead, striking out instinctively to where we could smell the land.

Of Rupert, Alex and Bran, I saw no more for the time being. Every nerve in me was strung up in the effort for self-preservation. When we had first washed over the side, Flopsy had given a strangled mew of fear and clawed desperately into my mane, where her paws were still hooked. I could still feel the light weight of her on my back, but it was no longer a warm weight, just a little frozen lump. But, somehow, her presence gave me courage to struggle on where perhaps if I had been alone I might have given in. Our lives seemed bound up in a series of events: first one of us saved the other, and was then saved.

I cannot tell if it were really so, only I know that if it had not been for the resolution to save my pal I should not be here where I am now in the golden sunset of life, at peace, and able to preach my philosophy of hope to all who journey out to do battle with their fate.

On and on we swam, and once or twice I felt below me hard sand. Then I was on my feet once more, though around

me were yet tossing white caps on the green waters. I was on
a far-flung spit of sand, uncovering at low tide and now
swiftly appearing through the water. Soon I had staggered
out of the waves altogether and was on firm ground once
more, ground that did not groan and roll and wallow.

But I was weary to death. I shivered and my sides heaved;
my breath rattled and wheezed in my throat as I stood
staring at the low bleak borderland of the Essex saltings—
then the loneliest, most forbidding stretch of country in all
that coast. Sedges and marsh-weed, rushes and sea-lavender
grew upon those forgotten wastes, islanded by the tides.
Mile upon mile of barren flatness with no sight of home or
steading, no cheerful curl of smoke to mark the homes of
men. And, for the first time in my life, I longed for men,
longed for the rough sound of their voices, for the firm grip
of their hands, and for the mastery of their intellect. Had a
man come then and claimed me, I had gone with him in
happy willingness and never fretted nor shown ugly temper,
my spirit tamed by my great need.

How differently things might have turned out for me!
But I was alone. Presently I felt Flopsy half jump, half
tumble from my back, and then in the first beams of the
rising sun she stretched and stretched, forepaws, then back-
paws, as if to get the tingling ache right out of them.

It was a beautiful enough world now that it was all bathed
in the forgiving sunlight. There were banks of soft green
and deep blue where the grass dykes and sea-lanes ran,
wandering endlessly to the horizon. Against the cold early
blue, clouds of wild duck rose clamouring from the reeds to
circle aloft, their racing shadows flying over the ground like
soundless bats.

I whinnied softly as I felt the pale warmth of the sunshine
on my coat and all at once things did not look so bad. I
even saw some tufts of sweet grass and stretched my neck

down to nibble them. Flopsy sat on a low mound and began to clean herself, a piece of work that was likely to keep her busy for some time to come.

And so from the sea we were saved, and now began a new period of our lives together. Grazing for me and hunting for Flopsy kept us interested; she was quite equal to keeping herself on the teeming wild life all about her. We wandered slowly inland until we were out of sight of the tumbling, sun-jewelled seas; only the faint sound of their turmoil still came to us as a pulsing murmur. When the first evening came we were luckier than we could have hoped—the vagabond horse and the homeless cat! Cattle were turned out on these wastes and in places rough shelters had been devised for them if caught in storms. One of these, partly wrecked but still standing, had its back to the prevailing westerlies of this bitter coast. I was thankful for it as I slept there, with Flopsy at my feet in the dear old way.

We were out with the first light next morning, and once or twice I missed the cat as I wandered, grazing peacefully. She returned to my side each time, but with an increasing lapse of time between, until at last she came no more and I knew she had taken to the wild life, as cats will. I mourned for the warm comfort of her presence, and it was then that the first bitterness against men began to grow in my heart, for I felt that they were to blame all along. It was a man-made world of events which had brought me here.

Mind you, I was still unspoilt then. I was not yet the vicious man-eater I became through ill-usage. But that night, just as I had settled in my shelter, I heard a storm of galloping and started out, quivering with fear. Eyes dilated and nostrils flaring, Alex and Bran came racing across the flats, leaping the sea-ditches. Blood and foam flecked their sides and panic rode them. Panic is infectious, and with ancient herd instincts fired I joined them at once, tuned to their mood in a wild gallop for safety, even though I did not know from what we were flying.

On and on we raced, and the excitement of that abandoned charge keyed me up till I felt I could have overcome anything that tried to stop me. At long last, far from my usual haunts and in wilder country than I had yet found, country which was a tangle of bramble-vines, our gallop became a canter and then a walk. Sweating and with heaving flanks, I began to think that we had all been acting rather foolishly.

"What are we running from?" I asked Bran.

With his ungroomed coat and wild eyes, he was a very different creature from the sleek beauty who had gone on board at Harwich. "From the stones!" he cried. "The stones, the awful stones! The boys thought it fun—they felt no doubt like bold Western hunters. They wanted to see us gallop and so they threw stones. Alex here is badly hurt, for one struck him over the eye."

"What boys?" I asked stupidly. I must confess that the very thought that there might be men or boys near me was the most heartening thing I had ever felt.

"The boys, the drovers who round up the cattle—wild, half-grown lads roaming the marshes." Alex snorted and stamped. "We are as good as they. I am even better. Men trace my pedigree back for generations and yet these louts think they have the right to hunt us!" His eyes flashed and he arched his neck and shook his withers so that his mane rippled. "If they do it again I shall turn on them," he cried; "but they stampeded us this time. If that is the way men treat us here they had better look out!"

I did not answer, for I did not realise then that all youths are not Andreas, and somehow I craved my old life of service. So next day I made my way further inland than I had yet been and I stood on a low hillock and gazed away over

the dykes, my ears pricked forward eagerly. The soft winds
blew my mane about me as I stood there listening to the
wailing of the peewits. I saw a company of lads, big, rough
fellows with great heavy drovers' sticks in their hands. They
had lowering, unintelligent faces and there was a wild quality
in their voices and clothes which ought to have warned me.
And yet why? Old Gipsy Jacko lived in his brambled rags
all the time I knew him, and yet his mind was as keen, his
love as great as any man's.

The boys set up a shout when they saw me. "There's one
of they hosses," one cried.

"No, it ain't. Thass a new one! That's bigger nor them
others. Make him run! With those legs he oughter be a sight!
Make him run!"

The cry was echoed by the others in hoarse delight. I had
never been mild-tempered, as you know, and had always
immediately resisted what I took to be injustice, even to the
length of snapping. But I could not believe they meant this.
I had lived long enough among men to know that I was very
valuable and I clung desperately to the hope that one of
them would take me to some farm, where once again I could
be owned and cared for.

So I trotted eagerly towards them and they fell back in
sudden terror. They liked to have wild things run from them;
it gave them a sense of power.

"Stop him, Alf," the first craven yelled, and himself
stooped to gather up some stones. Next second they came
singing round my ears like wild wasps and one struck me full
on the bony part just above my velvet nose. The pain and
the agonising surprise of it made me start away, to stand
quivering.

"Thass right! Make him run," came again the cruel yell,
and more stones flew.

My heart was so full of the misery of this betrayal of my

trust I could not think clearly, but turned and fled, my hoofs scattering the sandy soil. Away and away I ran, my grief changed queerly to fear, as it had done, no doubt, with Bran and Alex. When I stayed my wild flight at last I was so spent and miserable I had no heart even to nibble some grass for my dinner, but stood in the shelter of some wind-torn scrub, head down, deserted and alone.

I must not weary you with the tale of those winter months, which changed me from what I had been to a vicious animal who was quite likely to be shot on sight as a danger to the countryside. We three were evidently known of by now, and more and more boys joined the first little band in the heady delight of chasing us and flinging stones. They grew bolder and would stalk us, creeping up on us from our lee side so that we should not wind them. And we, in our turn, changed very quickly into the same wild creatures that our ancestors had been. Very soon our instincts told us to rest where one of us could always be on sentinel duty; we learned to watch the low skyline for moving heads.

One by one, through lack of man's attention to them, we cast our shoes; our coats thickened, and we were in all respects one with the wild ponies of which Bluegrass had told me. But what finally made my break with men was the incident about Flopsy. She came back to me now and again to snuggle against my legs, crooning who knew what little tales of her adventures and delights, for I fancy she had taken up with some great tom-cat who stalked the saltings in search of life, his home far distant, perhaps, on some farm in the Essex cornlands.

One day those louts caught her. How, I don't know, for she was fleet of foot as a wild bunny, but they did. They held her while a council met to decide what they should do with her, what sport they could have with her who had never harmed them. I don't know what they planned, but there was a roar of delight. A knife flashed as I watched from the shelter of a low mound. They did not know I was near. Something seemed to break in me then! Something died which up to that time had been a little warm flame in my heart. With a bound I was in among them at last. I had never been so near. Flopsy dropped from their grip and raced unhurt like a streak of yellow light. And then I began! I got my teeth into the ragged coat of the biggest of those hulking brutes and I swung him off his feet and shook him as Flopsy used to shake her rats at Honeysuckle Cottage.

He screamed for help, but his comrades, cowards as all bullies are, were on the run already. I dropped him and kicked his body to one side, then, with red eyes, made after the others. It was the other way about now. It was I who was seeing them run. But they could not get away from me. I kicked and shook them all, then, snorting, stood off to watch them limp away cringing and crying. After that, it was I who was the hunter. It was I who stood up to look for them and the first sight of their faces was my signal for a charge.

Often, Bran and Alex joined me, and we became the famous wild horses of Essex about which men wrote to the papers. Great naturalists argued about us, some tried to come out and see us, but we were through with men and we hunted them all gloriously out of our territory.

The hatred of men born in my heart when I saw my cat pal helpless in their hands grew and strengthened until even Andrea's memory faded from me. It became my joy to hunt, to run red-eyed after a flying foe. Always, as I have told you, nervous and apt to start at shadows, this my defect seemed to make me worse. I seemed now to be able to remember only the evils in my life: the cruelty of Barsard, the carelessness of the boy groom, and the menace of those big cats at the circus. I was a fighting wild horse and man was my enemy!

CHAPTER SEVENTEEN

THE RED DANE

THE SPRING, which had always come with a balm of peace and promise to an awakening world, brought me only fresh spirits and no softer gentle warning of what I had lost. I must confess that I was the wildest of the three of us, and sometimes we had half-mock battles among ourselves, trials of strength, when we raced with each other and bit and snapped in earnest.

I missed the two in the late spring and I never knew what came of them, but I suspect that some clever man with more brains than most saw his opportunity of getting a high-mettled mount for no more trouble than the catching of it—though I shrewdly suspect that both Alex and Bran would give plenty of trouble before they bowed their heads once more to bit and bridle.

But no bad times last for ever and things are always changing. As sure as the catkins blow in April lanes so certain it is that in another six months the gales will strip the trees of their autumn mantle of reddened leaves. The winter frosts give a kiss of death to the worn-out honey-bees, but the song of the January winds gives way to the praise of happy larks.

I now met a man who made a great change in my life and was my first step back along the wild road I had come. As I found out all about him later I may as well condense it now into a description of him to save time, so that you can tell a little what he was like.

Men called him the Red Dane, the Mad Dane, and many other names because they in their silly way were afraid of him. All alone he lived at Dane's Folly, on the Essex marshes, a farmstead once prosperous. He had come from foreign lands, so they said, and himself built the rambling house with its queer step-gables.

All he touched had prospered, but the country folk whispered among themselves, for they noticed that no swallows ever built below the eaves of Dane's Folly. He brought his pretty little wife with him, a girl who could only lisp English but whose very laughter was sunshine. The story goes that even the shy rabbits would come and nibble at her fingers when she called them. But the bleak cold, the damp cold she had never met before, crept into her and froze her and one year she passed away with the spring snows. After that, nothing went well.

The Red Dane wandered about his acres, a gloomy man whose eyes had hardened strangely. His temper became short and his farm-hands left him. They had the foot-and-mouth one year at Toosy and no one else within twenty miles suffered. But they say that the dreaded fires burned at Dane's Folly and spread a lurid light to reflect in the marsh-pools. The chickens strayed, the cattle were cut off by high tides. His chaff-cutter was silent in the barn, his ploughs rusted away, the fatal charlock spread over his fallow-land.

But his greatest trial was to see all about him hurt or in trouble while he personally was immune like an iron fence-post in a forest fire; the flames eat bush and furze and waving tree but leave the metal untouched. He was gaunt as an oak-stem, all its softer parts rotted away to leave only the toughest knotted heart-wood. He stalked in patient fortitude to and from his fields alone, cultivating the small patch which gave him the roots he needed. Often he must have wondered wistfully why he was outcast. He had not even a dog. In early mornings he took his gun and

went hunting for his dinner, lonely as was the legendary
Robinson Crusoe of which the small children talk.

But his spirit was the same as mine, unconquerable, and it
was one of the queer tricks which life plays us that he and I
were fated to meet. Without doubt he must have heard the
stories of the wild horses and interest must have pricked him
for the first time in many years. Even then, we might not
have met if it had not been for Flopsy. The wild tom-cat she
had taken up with was originally from Dane's Folly, but he
too had yielded to some queer instinct and left the place.
Now and again he returned to thieve from its great kitchen
if his hunting had gone ill. Once or twice, I know, Flopsy
followed him and watched him calm-eyed from the over-
grown bushes of the neglected garden while he skulked
round to the back.

Following Flopsy one day in anxious curiosity and fear
for her safety, I came out on higher ground and saw before
me the place about which so many legends have grown in
the years since.

There was a hush upon it. No chuckle of barnyard chick
broke the silence, no dog marked the afternoon watch with
sonorous, bell-like notes. The paint had not been renewed
since the place had first been built and was chipped and
rusted round the window-hasps. Nettles flourished their
first forests thickly about the walls, no sting as yet in their
sappy growth.

I felt nervous and fearful—why, I did not know. It
seemed a long, long time since I had seen a house, or the
drift of curtains at windows, even if these curtains were un-
washed and undarned.

Then a side door opened and a man came out with a
bucket. Tall and thin he was, with the face of a hawk and
queer red eyes, which matched his sandy hair; on the whole
it was a pleasant, patient face.

He saw me and stared incuriously, as if he were well used to seeing things which were not there. But as *I* saw *him*, all my man-hate roused and I began to paw the ground and snort. He started, knowing now that I must be real. There was a high stone wall between us, so I could not get at him, but he took a step forward and then paused to stare again.

"The wild horse," I heard him mutter in English, and then in slow admiration, "Beauty, you beauty!"

He came to the stone wall, but when he reached it I was twenty yards away, having wheeled in proud disdain of him and all he stood for. He rested his arms on the wall top and leaned his chin on his clenched fists. His strange red eyes held me as he stared and stared. I moved restlessly, wondering why I did not break away and race to safety.

"Ah, come to me, beauty," the man pleaded, but I shook myself and pranced, my eyes white ringed, my ears back.

He shrugged and turned away and I thought he had given up, but I did not know the Red Dane. He crossed to a gate in the side of the wall, opened it, and stepped out to come to me. He did not hurry; he did not seem to know fear.

As for me, I was bewildered. Why didn't I charge him as I now charged all men I saw? He had no weapon, not even a stick, and he did not stop to pick one up, though there were plenty about. He went on talking to me too and many of the words were strange, but I knew pretty well what he meant.

"I shall call you Trold, as they say it in my country," he said slowly. "Fairy horse—no—pixie horse—or does elf-horse translate it better? Come then, Trold; you are mine!"

I managed to break away from the spell of his voice, and gallop off when he got closer, but I was sweating and felt queerly uncertain. When I was a quarter of a mile away I paused and began to graze, wondering as I did so what had become of Flopsy and her tom. Some instinct made me raise my head to look along my back trail and I really did get a shock this time, for there was the Red Dane, unhurried still but relentlessly walking after me as if he had all day to waste, which perhaps he had. The sight did something to me, for it woke fear in me and I determined to get as far from him as I could.

This time I galloped on and on over ground I had not crossed before, leaping the wide tide-ditches, or splashing through them when I could not take them. On I went, my one desire being to shake off this man I hated and feared. The cooling evening breathed with sweetened breath when at last I paused for rest. Long I stood with head up, nervously watching the way I had come.

But I had won this first round, for the young moon gleamed down on desertion and the only sound was the keening wind in the stunted bushes. After that, for many days, I kept away from Dane's Folly and nearer the sea-coast. But some fatal fascination led me to follow Flopsy there once more. The nearer I got, the more terrified I became and the blacker my rage that in some secret way man could still draw and dominate me.

The Red Dane, quiet and determined as ever, walked me off his land. Something in his dogged, relentless pursuit scared me. I could have turned and savaged him, but I did not.

"I will have you for mine yet, Trold," he called to me as if I could speak and answer him. Men get into a habit of thinking aloud who live too long alone. "You are mine, you know!"

He did get me in the end, with a clever trick. There was at a little distance a barn of his out on the saltings and here he began to leave food. Not food for me, mind you! He was far too clever for that. But he had marked that in our rough life Flopsy and I were stable-mates, so he left food for her. Her kittens were growing in her and she was always hungry, so she went there daily and her tom-cat shadowed her and crooned to her as she ate.

I hated to see her accept the Red Dane's food, but no harm came to her, and she began spending most of her time there, for he had spread an old carriage-rug on straw for her. Often and often as he came from the house carrying an old tin dish with some tasty supper he had contrived for her he would surprise me lurking near, watchful.

I would make off with a flourish of heels, but now he no longer appeared to notice me. Not that his iron purpose had altered by so much as an inch. The old doors to the barn were never closed. They looked too rotten ever to be moved again; the rich green mildew growing on the cross-bars was like living emeralds. But in this I was wrong; those doors were not rotten at all.

One day when I heard the old familiar sounds of the new-born kittens, Flopsy's brood of loving happiness, I ventured into the gloom, stepping as carefully as if ice lay beneath my feet. She put up her face to be loved and lipped, and I stood over her remembering—oh, such strange half-forgotten moments of long ago!

The slam of the big doors and the jar as the bar dropped into place woke me to reality. With a scream of wild fear such as my forebears no doubt gave on the prairies and steppes I turned to fly away from the trap, but it was too late. I was in it! The Red Dane had got me!

Very well, I would kill him when he came. I trotted up and down restlessly, turning at each end of the barn to return again, head up, tail switching, prowling as the great cats used to do. When I heard him coming I was in such a lather of excitement that I hardly knew what I was doing.

He did not come in through the big doors as I had ex-

pected, but went up the hay ramp outside and in at the first
floor where the hay was kept, for the next moment there he
stood at the trapdoor looking down at us.

"Now you *are* mine, Trold," he said slowly. "And we
will soon get to know each other. I feel that we think the
same about a lot of things. I have brought your supper. I
do not starve those who belong to me and there has been
no one 'belonging' for so long!"

He began to come down the ladder and then I saw that
he had a pan of oats. I had not tasted anything like oats for
so long and had become quite used to the naturally dried
hay of the winter dykes, for there had been no lack of eating
on the marshes.

But I backed off warily. He took no further notice of
me, but brought a pail of water and some good hay. Then,
turning his back on me, he went over to Flopsy and fondled
her so that the silly cat purred at him in rich content. She
had evidently met him and grown quite used to him.

He was a brave man, that Dane. But I could no more
have attacked him as he stood there with his back to me
loving my pal than I could have flown. Probably he knew
it. He left us, but I ate little and slept less. If, that night
when the storm-wind howled across the marshes and rain
drummed on the roof, if the thought crossed my mind that
I was very comfortable in shelter, I felt humiliated and as if
I had betrayed myself.

Morning came, but before it was light the Dane was there.
He made no attempt to groom me. He knew no doubt just
how far it was wise to go, but he brought me more food,
though not too much, and he tidied my bedding. I was, of
course, at the other end of the barn while he did it, watching
him with eyes as red as his own. Then he put down a dish
for Flopsy and filled it with bread-and-milk. Tom-cat was
not there. He had made off at the first sight of the kittens.

"There will be a little life now in the old place," the man whispered joyfully as he counted the kittens. "Drown you? No, I wouldn't drown one of you if I were to be paid in golden sovereigns for doing it!"

Then away he went again and left us. I had a horrid feeling that I did not hate him quite so much as I had done; this realisation made me restless and uncertain of myself. I caught myself actually listening for him when he came that evening, but when he was there I still wanted to hate him as badly as ever.

It was on the third day that matters came to a head between us. He came in for the first time through the big doors and he left one side wide open. I could hardly believe my eyes. Outside it was a pleasant morning, with all the fresh promise of a sweet day. The rolling meadows in front of the barn just before the marsh began were a sheet of flowers, buttercups, lady's smock, bedstraw, and the rosy first leaves of the sorrel. I gathered myself up for a rush for freedom! When I saw my chance, I took it!

But as I passed him, off my guard in my excitement, he leaped at me, agile as any of the artistes of the circus-ring. His iron-strong hands were wrapped in my flying mane; he laughed and was upon my back before I knew where I was. Together we passed out into the open. He was riding me— my enemy was on my back and was urging me forward with heel and hand. I was wild with rage and I raced away over field and dyke and swampy tract, over hedgerow and his bit of cabbage-land, away and away as fast as I could gallop.

It felt strange enough to be carrying the weight of a rider again like this, especially without shoes on my feet. I must get rid of him! He was just bearable if he did not touch me, but let me shelter in his barn and eat his food. But this— this was unforgivable! At the same time I could not help thinking that it *might* have been Andrea. They rode with the same easy grace and skill. It was the first time in many weeks that I had thought of Andrea and I felt queerly ashamed. Perhaps if I could only get rid of my rider I might feel better.

Out of the past came a memory of Bluegrass and the lesson he had taught me so long ago.

"You may want to get rid of your rider sometime," Bluegrass had said. "Just put your feet like this—so—take a short stiff jump and come down *so*! Never forget that, son!"

We were a long way from Dane's Folly by now, heading inland. I remember noticing a farmhouse ahead and I heard the old familiar sound of a dog's bark. But Bluegrass's words were ringing in my head. I bucked there and then, not very successfully, because I had never before tried it.

"Look out!" the Red Dane called out sharply. "Steady down, Trold!"

The sound of his voice made me worse. Again and again I bucked. I had never felt such an exciting feeling as this: the shock it gave even to me, the pounding, relentless thrill of it. I could quite understand Bluegrass's stories of buckers who could never be cured but who took to the habit as men take to cards or drink.

I felt the Red Dane sway and lose his balance and I knew I was winning. One more effort and I heard him fall behind me. I wheeled to trample on him. But as I saw him I braked my rush so swiftly that I was nearly down on my haunches. He was half sitting, half lying against a low bush, and his face even through its all-year tan was paper white. He was not lying naturally, for one leg seemed twisted. He was completely defenceless and at my mercy.

CHAPTER EIGHTEEN

BACK TO THE WORLD

I STOOD there snorting over him, my eyes wide and staring. He looked up at me and there was not the faintest hint of fear in his red eyes or in his voice, though his face twisted as he spoke.

"All right, you win," he said, shrugging and then wincing. "Run away back to your marshes. Away with you to your freedom. I daresay you value it as much as I do mine!" He gestured with his hand and the dullest mind could have understood him. "Get along! Be off!"

I began to tremble, because I simply did not know why I couldn't move off. Here was the thing for which I had been fighting; I'd won fairly and yet now that I had it I could not take it. The man watched me, amazement flashing across his face. Then he began to laugh!

In spite of the pain of his broken leg, the Red Dane sat there and laughed and laughed at the absurdity of anything wanting to stay near him. I think I told you that human laughter always has a very queer effect on me. It makes me uncomfortable and restive. Not that he cared what effect it had on me. I felt in his presence that there was no pretence about him. He was not showing fear simply because he was not afraid and he was laughing because he really did see something odd in the situation. I felt that he and Andrea were much more alike in their outlook than I could have guessed.

"Go along with you," the Red Dane cried again, and he flourished his arm. "My dreams of having a bit of life again at the old place were so much empty moonshine!"

His voice was very tired all at once. You may think it very stupid of me, but I felt that I could not leave him, even if he were my enemy—and was he? I could not help him, but humans could. Men helped each other, I knew. Had I not ridden wildly once in hot-foot haste to bring aid to my own loved master? I pranced in uncertain misery, torn with all sorts of feelings I never thought I possessed.

Then the dog barked again at that farm and I tossed up my head, ears pricked forward to listen. I swayed away from where the man still lay, and trotted a few steps away, then wheeled and trotted back. His amused eyes were on me and I could not bear their look a moment longer.

This time I went off down the road as once I had raced to fetch Gipsy Jacko, only this time I went alone. Then it had been for the boy I loved; now it was for the man I hated.

There was a woman planting out leeks on a nicely smoothed bit of ground and when she saw me she cried: "Mercy on us!" and threw away the trowel and bolted in at her back door, while the farm-dog went raving mad. But her man was of tougher fibre. She had hardly disappeared and no doubt gasped out a tale of a wild horse right in the back garden; then he was outside to see for himself.

I whinnied to him and he stared and stared.

"And don't you come too close, you wicked-looking thing," he warned. "Sarah, keep well away, wife!"

I trotted away a little piece up the road, then paused, looked back, and whinnied again.

"This needs looking into," the man muttered. "But I'll take no chances. Goodness only knows what tricks the brute might be up to. Sarah, wife, bring me my duck-gun. If he starts anything, I'll scare the life out of him!"

Armed, he followed me out into the rough road, but he kept a wary distance. I did not care. I had got what I wanted and now started off with purpose. When I paused

E

to look back he paused too and swung his gun to his shoulder, but I ignored that and led on again. When he came in sight of the Red Dane, he set up a great shouting.

"Per Edlund, neighbour!" He sounded quite hoarse with excitement. "What's this, what's all this? Is this your beast? I didn't know, neighbour, that you'd any cattle to touch this. Are you hurt?"

The Red Dane laughed dryly. "I've crocked myself a bit, sure enough, Bob. You'll have to get some men to carry me, and I hope your old Jimmy is still the bone-setter he was. The horse——? Well, I *thought* he was mine, but I expect I was wrong. I mostly am!"

"Don't you be bitter, man," the farmer warned. "A lot of your troubles are your own making, shutting yourself away from those who could help. Shall I catch your beast first?"

"Catch him—catch *him*?" Again the Red Dane laughed. "No fear; let him go free."

I waited for no more but galloped off, kicking up my heels joyfully. I was free again! I owed no allegiance to any man. I would go as far away as I could from Dane's Folly and the very memory of the man who had caught me. Flopsy would soon rejoin me when her kittens were old enough to fend for themselves.

All that day I roamed and did as I wished, grazed or galloped as I had done in the past weeks, drank at a stream which emptied itself into the marshes. I rolled on the lush grass and played about like any colt. But right down inside me I was not truly happy. I was sore and angry. I might be free in one sense, but I could not get the thought of that man out of my head; the sound of his voice still rang in my ears; I could see his quelling glance in every cloud-shadow. I hated but respected him.

I would just go and take a look at Flopsy's kittens and

make sure they were all right and that no prowling fox could get into the barn. There was no harm in going up to the place and merely peering in. The Red Dane could not hurt me, for he would never know and he could not get about, anyway. I did not go back all at once. Somehow I would not allow even to myself that I wanted more than all things in the world to have a good man's hand groom and pat me again, and a man's strength to govern me.

Bit by bit I found myself wandering north-west in the general direction of the lonely farm and next evening I was actually grazing within a hundred yards of it. I did look in at the kittens, but I didn't go into the building. They were squealing and tumbling about on the rug the man had given them, but Flopsy was not there. She was out hunting for meals. Disappointed not to see her, I looked across at the house. It was, of course, even more silent than usual; the only light was the golden square of an upstairs window. But queerly enough I was happier than I had been for weeks. I came back next morning and through the next few weeks I was never very far away. I even ventured into the barn now and again and helped myself to the hay, a large mass of which had been forked down out of the loft the last time the Red Dane had been up there.

One day, some weeks later, when I was grazing on the unkept lawn before the house, I heard the side door open. I took no notice, for I was quite used to hearing and seeing the woman from the farm, Sarah, coming and going, for she was housekeeping for the Red Dane, her neighbour. I often saw a face watching me from the window upstairs and had supposed it was she. So I did not look up and was very much startled when a familiar voice spoke.

"Wildling Trold! Then you are still with us?"

I tossed up my head and leaped aside, wheeled, and trotted away, trembling violently. The Red Dane was thinner and looked greyer in his face and he was walking with the help of a stout stick, but his eyes were the same, with the same red spirit in them. He stood there so long gazing at me that I began to paw the ground in my nervousness. His eyes naturally lowered to watch my action. Then he stilled queerly and stared.

"How long, Trold, have you been free?" he said. "No shoes! This is a very strange matter!"

He began to hobble towards me, but I could no more have galloped away than I could have stood on my head. When he was quite near he laid down his stick, bent and picked up one of my feet, cradling it against his knee. I looked down at his bowed back, his rough brown tweed coat and bared head. It was all fantastic, but something inside me was singing with happiness. I stood as good as gold while he made his examination.

"We must put this right, Trold," he said firmly. "The ground has not been too hard for you and the horn is sound as a bell. Up, boy, up; we'll look at all of them. Yes, the quicker you have on honest shoes again the better, if you are to go out into the world to work once more. Eh, Trold? I must write to someone and try to trace you and where you come from. I have no claim on you really, except that I like you and would like to keep you!"

I may say here that I heard he did write but could not find out anything, so I suppose that Mr. Dubois had long ago given me up as lost and gone back to his own country.

That day I had corn to eat in the barn and the man groomed me. A little real peace crept warmly into my heart. He and I were of the same mettle and all was well. What I did not realise was that it was only towards himself that I had changed. I had not, unhappily, lost my new feeling of hatred and revolt against men. Some spirit seemed to have been born in me in all those lonely weeks of cruel hunting and stone-slinging by those boys, a spirit of dull resentment. I found this out only the next day.

"Come along, Trold," the Red Dane called me. "The farrier is here. Now we will soon have you right!"

He was looking a bit tired and I think his leg was aching a bit, for he had been doing too much work all morning getting a roaring fire going in his little forge ready for the shoesmith. He put a halter on me and led me into the shelter quietly enough.

But when I saw another man there all my old madness returned. Back went my ears; I bared my lips off my teeth, and I know my eyes must have looked dreadful. I snatched up my head and tore the rope out of the Red Dane's hands, then snapped viciously at the farrier, who, poor man, was taken by surprise and barely got out of reach in time.

"Hold hard!" Edlund cried, jumping to my head. But I wheeled at that instant, knocking him down in my excitement, and leaped out into the open, where I stood poised for flight, not quite certain whether or no, if I galloped away then, I should ever come near Dane's Folly again.

The Red Dane came out limping, but in my worked-up mood I hardly noticed or cared. I think he must have realised how desperate the case was, for he shrugged and turned away. The farrier packed up his things and departed grumbling that that was the first time a horse had turned on him and he in the trade these fifty years. He seemed quite upset about it, but I just did not care!

When all was quiet again, Edlund led me back into the shed and he put the shoes on me himself, for he had been used to doing it in the old days—I could tell that. I fancy it cost him a good deal, for he looked rather done up when he had finished. After the joyous lightness of my freedom the heavy shoes were hateful, but it could not be helped.

After that, I often caught the Red Dane looking at me

with a puzzled expression on his face as if I were a great problem to him. One day when the doctor paid a last routine visit I heard the two men talking. They were walking back to the horse and trap waiting by the road gate. I had kept out of sight when he drove up.

"If I can't ride for all that time," Edlund was saying, "the horse can't stay here getting wilder every day. I feel responsible for the poor brute, but I don't know where to send him. He won't be happy till he is working again and has got over this hate business."

"You think he will get over it?" the other man asked dubiously.

"He's all right with me," the Red Dane pointed out. "But this is no place to cure him. We must get him back again among other horses and men for his own sake. I tell you I know it will be all right. I'm doing it for him, for I should ask nothing better than to keep him!"

"Well, don't come to me when the damage is done," the doctor said. "Why don't you send him to Windywold, old Major Lyle's place? You used to know his headman, Tom Cartright. He's cured more vicious horses than there are days in a year!"

Edlund seemed very much struck by this. "If Cartright is in it, it will be all right," he said emphatically. "That's an idea worth brooding. Something good might hatch. One thing I know is that the cat will have to go too. She's the only other link Trold seems to have with plain common-sense. But I will have the kittens for mine own! Four fine fat ginger kittens! The place will be quite lively."

"You are a strange man," the doctor mused, and he drove away.

I was most uneasy at all this talk. Why couldn't I stay? The lovely flat marshland held a fascination for me. I was not at all sure that I wanted to go back to work, but I had

no choice and this in itself made me bitter—not against the
Red Dane, though! I should always feel a warmth of
genuine liking for him in the years to come.

So that is how it came about that one day in late June of
that year Edlund himself led me gently along the drowsy
lanes to a small station, where he put me on the train.
Flopsy in a large basket was put in with me and I stood
there fretting and foaming while he talked to me and patted
me.

"Be a good fellow, Trold," he advised. "I have written
to Cartright explaining it all and he will meet you. You
will have a wonderful time if you try to please. They have
a great estate and many horses, and a town house and mews
in Mayfair. It is best as it is. I hate losing you, for you
have brought me back my love of life. I think, no, I know I
shall make Dane's Folly prosper now. Perhaps in the spring
next year the swallows will come to me. It was the will to
get on and do my best which had died in me when Marta
went. But now things will be so different!"

One last pat and then he got down. The doors were closed
and barred and the train began to move. I was once more
going out into the unknown to a strange place. But nearly
the darkest patch in my life was over and done with for ever.

CHAPTER NINETEEN

WINDYWOLD

MY LIFE seemed to be like that—always moving on somewhere. Nothing stayed settled for very long. I never saw the Red Dane or the Essex saltings again. The salt winds and the sandwort and the sea-lavender are only a fading memory with me now.

I sometimes wonder as I doze in my cosy shelter here that if I could go back just for another glimpse of it all would I find all my life's halting-places still there? Are the dandelions growing in the circus-yard, do the rats still thump and squeal in the stables at Honeysuckle Cottage now that Flopsy's ruling paw is gone for ever, does the Red Dane till his flat lands with new horses and ploughs and disc-harrows, while his increasing stocks of fine red cattle roam the saltings? I expect progress has swept it all away.

We ran into Peterly, the station for Windywold, at two in the morning and my box was backed on to a siding. My reputation had gone ahead of me, for some food and water were hastily thrust in to me and the door banged to again. The porters were taking no chances. Poor Flopsy got nothing, but she had had some good baked crusts, of which she was fond, put in her hamper by the Red Dane.

The sudden flash of the station-lamps dazzled me after the gloom of my box; I was feeling rather sore and unhappy, so I relieved my feelings by kicking round pretty considerably. I kicked my water bucket over with a crash, and the

noise did me a lot of good. When the rats had worried me
I had kicked in an honest attempt to rid myself of the pests;
now I kicked purely out of temper!

Was no one ever coming to fetch me? Had they all forgotten me? Should I stay boxed up here for the rest of my
life? I wavered between panic and black temper. Then, at
long last, I heard voices, one a mild, quiet one with a little
easy laugh in it.

"Yes, of course," the man was saying; "the one time
when it was important that I should get here early I was
held up. Oh, he's in here, is he—the horse that they wrote
to the Major about? Move off, please; I'll get him out alone.
If he's really as fidgety as they say he'll be better if he
doesn't see too many new faces."

Fidgety! There was a nice understatement for you.
Raving mad was nearer the mark. Daylight blinded me as
the door opened, and there stood a little man barely five feet
tall with the bandy legs of an old jockey and a smooth face
the colour and texture of harness-leather. He had the smallest
eyes of any man I ever saw, and they kept up an incessant
twinkling even when he was looking grave, as if they were
little points of black fire under his lids.

With no fuss or hurry, but without one second's hesitation,
he was up the ramp and had undone my fastenings and was
leading me out.

"Bring the cat," he called over his shoulder to one of the
men.

But as soon as my feet were on the safe cobbles of the
railway-yard, I reared, almost swinging Cartright off his
bent legs.

"Steady there, steady!" he warned. "It's no good looking
like that at me! You're not the first savage I've taught
manners. Keep your teeth to yourself, please!"

He ducked away from my vicious snap at his arm, then

shortened his grip on my rope. "You'll be tired of this before I am," he panted.

I doubted this. I reared again and enjoyed seeing the silly porters racing away from my flashing hoofs. I felt suddenly all hot with the mad determination to shake off those restraining hands, rear away from their hold, break it and him too if need be.

But there was a grim tenacity in the way Cartright worked. His dead weight every time I tried to rear was getting tiring and he was not wasting an ounce of strength himself, but letting me do all the hard work.

"Steady there, old boy. Calm down, Trold," he kept saying monotonously.

I backed, I danced, I reared, I tried to walk on two legs and bite at the same time, but he was as quick as a river-eel and I did not know where to have him. Somehow he was never there when my teeth snapped together, and this jarred me and made my head sing.

When one finds that all one's efforts are useless, one feels rather blank. So I stopped rearing aimlessly and contented myself with tossing my head and rolling my eyes, keeping my teeth bared for a chance attack. I resisted when he began leading me, then changed my mind and stepped after him.

"Got a horse-box for him?" one of the men called, but Cartright shook his head.

"It isn't far. It'll do him no harm to walk. Send the cat on by the carrier and see the poor brute has some milk!"

I thought his voice sounded queer now that I had time to stop and think about it, and when he laid his hand on my back I *knew*! Cartright was afraid of me. I'd been so busy playing up that I'd never realised that here was a case of iron will driving a shrinking body to do feats of supreme courage!

That was true of Cartright all over. Ordinarily happy with horses, he always felt like this with a mulish brute who was out to give trouble, but he never let it influence him by so much as a breath. All the other horses at Windywold who talked to me in the weeks to come agreed with my finding. His was a better and perhaps a rarer courage than the Red Dane's. Per Edlund had never, I should say, found anything which could wake fear in him. Cartright had found plenty! But he went grimly on with his purpose in spite of it, schooling voice and eye and hand to act naturally, so that only those with acute senses knew of his trials. I doubt if his fellow-men ever suspected a thing!

As for me, it quietened me but helped to make me very nervous. I did not know where to have him nor what he might do next. His reactions were not to be counted on. I fretted and pranced a bit, but after that went on fairly easily, though I noticed that all who met us took one hasty glance at me and then climbed into the hedge until we were by.

But Cartright continued to lead me along as if I were a harmless old cow and his example of disregard was infectious. Soon I was not even fretting, but looking about me to see what sort of country it was we were in. It was as different from Essex as it well could be: high-broken country, with towering, craggy hills clothed up and down their rangy length with thick beech-woods. Between them were lush deep valleys with farms and towns and old-world villages. The roads wound and twisted as they led up the shoulders, and suddenly one would see through a break in the rocks the far-flung landscape, dwarfed to insect-size by the height and distance. Then another plunge into the rustling glory of the great woods, where the sun was stained to emerald-green and the air was full of the sweet tang of rotted leaves.

Then our road plunged downward for over a mile into a wide valley cut by a flashing river. With the hills at its back the small township nestled. But just beyond was the rolling parkland of a great estate, where red deer grazed and peacocks strutted. Between the trees could be glimpsed the white stones of an Italian-style country mansion. At the back were the stables and farm and a fine artificial lake, where in winter the smart young people for miles around were allowed to skate.

We did not go through the town, but, skirting it, came to a long drive which led on between magnificent walnut trees. A lodgekeeper's cottage with blazing geraniums in its windows housed an old couple who looked after the comings and goings through the twenty-foot wrought-iron gates.

I remembered almost sadly how I had used to dream of such places and being owned by people with as much land and money as the Lyles had. Horses can dream of the future as much as men can. But life had not been all green grass and corn, and much of my early ambition to rise and be famous had died. But once in the great square yard at Windywold, surrounded by very modern stabling, I could not help my spirits rising just a bit. I felt a grateful warmth towards the memory of the Red Dane, whose actions had rescued me from a lonely, loveless life and had, so to speak, put me back in circulation again.

I was assuredly back amongst my own kind again! There was a bustle of movement, and the ringing and click of hoofs all about me. On the left, in a big paddock, a string of horses were being exercised by four grooms in white shirts and knee-breeches. A low murmur of voices on the right came from some stable-lads who were cleaning out the loose-boxes on that side of the yard, and chattering merrily to one another. A fine big pony was being groomed by a fresh-

faced lad, who whistled as he worked. Evidently Major
Lyle was a great horse-lover and rider. Not since the circus
days had I had so many of my own kind about me. I was
puzzled by the number of ponies, for I could see their heads
looking out over the doors of their loose-boxes.

At sight of Cartright every face brightened. I could not
help thinking that even the horses appeared pleased to see
him back and I realised how a man's drive and personality
can make him a little king in his own world.

"Stand back; I'll take him in," he called.

One of the boys opened the doors of my new home, and,
with a stamp of hoofs on the brick flooring, I entered. Cartright brought me food and water, heaped more straw for
me, and then very wisely left me to simmer down and rest.
It was the kindness and humanity of the little bow-legged
man that made him what he was.

"Is he a killer?" I heard one of the boys ask, with a catch
of excitement in his voice.

"Well, he's the hottest packet that's sailed in here this
many a day," the headman answered in his mild way. "If
he'd had his way we'd never have got here. But if he doesn't
settle down at Lyle's he'll settle nowhere! He can't be worse
than Blue King last year, and you know where he is now—
drawing a duke's carriage in London, and the finest, most
talked-of horse in the Park."

"How d'you do it, sir?" the boy asked, but the answer
was lost as the man moved away.

I stood thinking over all this for a long time and I found
out a number of things. The first was that, beautiful as
these modern buildings were, they were far from being ideal
from a horse's point of view. Lovely white glazed tiles
covered the walls and could be cleaned to spotlessness in a
few seconds by a hose, but they reflected a glare of light
which was very tiring. The stables were designed to be wide

and airy and there was no hint of the fumes that are so often there in old-fashioned buildings. But care had not been taken to ensure that draughts were excluded and there were little currents and cross-currents idling around all the time, gently chilling to a tired horse and very irritating. But the other thing I found out was that straw was not stinted, nor horse-blankets. I could see two beautiful clean rugs in my box, besides the nice light one I wore. All the appointments were on the same lines; money was not spared.

Then a string of ponies came in and stamped, each into his own box, so that our line of boxes was full. I laid back my ears at the noise, and trembled with a kind of nervous temper which was now usual with me when startled. I snapped in the direction of the pony on my right, but of course could not reach him. The top half of the partition was openwork iron, so that the horses could see each other and not get bored. It is the boredom of standing inactive in stables which starts many vices such as wind-sucking and crib-biting.

But the pony had plenty of grit. "Don't do that!" he said sharply. "You've no cause to act ugly at Windywold and I'll not stand any nonsense."

I was so amazed that I said nothing for a minute, but bared my teeth warningly. "You must think a lot of yourself," I then replied stiffly.

"I do! I'm Scotsman, the best of Major Lyle's polo-ponies. In fact, I'm head pony. It's a position of great trust. He brought the game back with him from India, they say, and he's made it famous in this corner of the world. Why, when the Windywold Polo Team meets any other, people come from as far as London and Edinburgh to see us. There's a big match next week and we're in hard training, I can tell you. I'm the more surprised that they put you in here, as we are generally kept *very* select and undisturbed, but I suppose there wasn't anywhere else for you!"

"I suppose not," was all I could find to say, for the little beast's cheek and self-confidence took my breath away. I turned away and nosed in my straw and pretended to take no further notice. But I was feeling a bit lonely and wished I had not been so high-handed. It was wonderful to be able to talk to one's own kind again, and I had spoilt it myself.

"That's all right," the cheery, cheeky voice began again. "Look, we'll say no more about it! Now, tell me all your story. I always get a good story out of a newcomer and from what I've heard you've had plenty of adventures."

"There's nothing to tell," I said sulkily over my shoulder as I reached up idly to nibble at the ironwork.

"Don't do that!" Scotsman said again, very sharply. "It's a horrible habit and it grows on you if not stopped at once. I can't have you infect the team with it. Those ponies will copy anyone they admire just as silly men do, and they admire you. They've been looking forward to your coming ever since we heard the Major say to Cartright to go and bring you home!"

In spite of myself I could not help feeling warmed by this interest. Bit by bit I stopped sulking and told my story, and Scotsman listened with flattering attention, prompting me when there were bits he couldn't understand.

"I'll say the circus sounds mighty fine," he said, blowing into his straw and stamping in his excitement. "But, brother, you have had a time of it! I don't wonder at your being a bit off-colour in the temper department. Where is this Flopsy now?"

"Coming," I answered, and it was a funny thing but at that moment she came. There had been voices in the yard and the creak of a hamper, but I had not heeded them. Now a shadow fell on me as she jumped up on the half-door, knowing with unfailing instinct exactly where I was. Next moment her great golden furry body was weaving about my legs and her purr was so loud and sonorous that it seemed to shake her with its vibrations. And suddenly I felt much better. Life was not so bad, after all, perhaps. A bad patch was behind me. There might be more bad patches ahead, but there also might be golden promise of happiness and peace in my old age. I began to wonder if I hated all men quite so much as I had thought.

At noon, Cartright himself came with my food. It was such a habit now to lay my ears back and snap whenever I felt that irritation of someone's being near me that I could not break it but sidled and no doubt looked very ugly. The knowledge that he was afraid of me did not help me, and I know that if he had shown openly by so much as the quiver of a finger how he felt I should have turned on him. I could not seem to help it! That hot resentment of anger flamed up in me like a tide.

But he never hesitated. He came into the box, talking all the time and moving with a slow deliberation that is so comforting to us horses, who are scared of quick, flashy movements. My dinner he put before me with his own hands, and it looked very good: crushed oats, and I could see the twinkle of salt on them. Delicious!

"Poor old chap, poor old Trold!" Cartright said quietly and laid his hand on my back. "Well, you've got your stable-mate now. A few weeks with us and you won't know yourself. Come, Trold, let it be peace between us. Look at me!"

He didn't of course know that I could understand him, but in spite of my flattened ears I was attracted by him. Yet I turned to try and stare him out with red-eyed determination. It was a battle of wills between us. Well, I would win!

I didn't! In those tiny eyes I read things which made me feel quite queer. There was a spirit there of which I knew nothing and could never know; a courage out of this world and a kindly love towards all living things.

"That's better," he whispered as I turned away in bewildered fear.

"And, you know, he's right," Scotsman said pleasantly before he buried his nose in his dinner. "Play the game and it'll all turn out all right in the end."

I was not quite convinced yet. It seemed hard to believe that friendly work and happy play awaited me. Surely behind must be the ugly things I had learned to expect: the thoughtless cruelty of lazy grooms and heedless boys, the hardships of seeking one's own food and being dependent on one's own wits for survival, the loneliness of the open marshes.

I was still nervous and jumpy, and the draughty stables worried me at night when the air cooled. I had never been in such a big loose-box before, but I liked the independence of it. Moving about late that evening after our ten o'clock hay, I caught my foot against the woodwork, and the hollow sound of the thump brought back to mind Honeysuckle Cottage and its miserable rat-haunted nights. Hot rage filled me at the remembrance and I kicked out again and again to prove to myself that the present, anyway, seemed to promise better things. I got tired of it in the end, for, rather to my surprise, no outraged man burst in on me to lay a whip about my ears. To have no audience, to feel I wasn't annoying anyone, rather took the edge off things.

Cartright was out in the yard at five the next morning and all his lads were about him, fresh-faced and eager for work. What was this man's magic? I was impressed and ashamed and really made an effort when he came to clean out and fill the water-buckets. With him was one of the lads,

Jim by name. I could see he didn't like coming too near me, but he had plenty of pluck.

"The more faces he sees and gets used to, the better," Cartright muttered. "It's all right, lad; I'm here!"

Supreme confidence of man! How could *he* help if I decided to be nasty? I rolled a warning eye at the lad, but he was so unlike the coarse brutes on the marshes, so jolly-looking and willing, that I just couldn't snap. When he bent to caress Flopsy I was won over. A new day had dawned for me!

CHAPTER TWENTY

THE GREAT FLOOD

But no nonsense was allowed at Windywold, as the next incident will prove. The next day was fine and warm again and this time I was groomed very well, till I tingled all over and felt ready to jump a six-bar gate. The tingle was in my feet too, so that I danced when led out to exercise.

"Magnificent beast," I heard Cartright say. "If he doesn't trace back to one of the three Arabians I'm not a headman of twenty years' standing."

The exercise was good and the day passed well enough, with Scotsman yarning of his beloved polo. That night Flopsy had settled down to sleep, but I was excited and wakeful, my head teeming with new fancies and ideas, my old life somehow much nearer than it had been for a long time. I had shown very little temper all day, except once or twice, when irritated by trivial happenings. I lashed out and snapped if a gadfly as much as buzzed past my ears.

But a feeling had begun to grow in my heart that I should in time outgrow even this. But that night I learned to respect Cartright as well as like him. The pleasant remembrance came back to me of the fun I had had kicking and drumming with my hoofs last night. No sooner had I thought of it than I backed and lashed out.

But, oh, what was this? A sharp prickling pain ran up my leg and left it hot and sore. Amazed and really angry, I lashed out again and again, the pain tingling in my skin. I then stood still for awhile thinking this one out.

"I knew he'd soon stop that," Scotsman said sleepily from the next box. "It's an old trick, but it always works!"

"What does?" I asked testily, while the sleepy ponies stirred restlessly at the disturbance, their straw beds rustling.

"Furze, of course," Scotsman observed. If ponies could chuckle as men do I should have said he did. "Cartright hung a fine bush just where it would do the most good. I've known it cure a kicker in one go! He's a cure for every vice, I believe. Now go to sleep, please, and let us all get some rest."

I was as humiliated and angry as a child would feel if its hand was slapped while it stole the sugar, but I acknowledged the justice of the cure and fair play always made me respond with fair service. So I did not kick any more, but settled down. At the back of my mind, however, was the nagging thought that I would have it out with Cartright in the morning. Was I a common horse that he thought he could cure me with a common trick? When daylight came I examined the bush and then I was really angry. A great brute of a bush of furze, it was, stiff with prickles, a very nasty thing!

I began to work myself into a state, as usual, and when I heard the headman's voice outside I arched my neck and got my teeth ready. He came in brisk and healthy as a spring wind, and, before I could do a thing, had picked up my off hind foot and was examining it for pricks! He meant to cure me for my own sake and everyone's comfort, but he was going to hurt me as little as possible.

You can't very well do anything to a man like that! At least, I couldn't. And when he came to my head and gave me a pat and said: "Steady on, Trold; we'll be famous friends yet," I suddenly forgot all my temper—turned and looked full at him and pushed against him lightly with my nose.

The joy and light that twinkled in his little eyes did me good, and then and there I realised that there was a bond between us *and that he was no longer afraid of me*! It was an unspoken agreement. He was strong-willed but just; I was strong-willed but had been hurt and frightened. We agreed to forget.

"And *that's* all right!" Scotsman said comfortably. "Mind you, I didn't blame you for temper after what you'd told me, but it's no good here. We just won't have it!"

That was a very happy summer and autumn and every day my temper got better and better. I began to feel as if I had lived at Windywold all my life. Major Lyle came into the stable-yard a day or two after the furze incident to look at the ponies, for the big match was very near. Cartright brought him to see me. The tall, thin, soldierly man stood appraising me, slapping the leg of his riding-boot with a small swagger-cane, and nodding.

"How's he shaping now, Cartright? He's a picture. Finest sight I ever saw and I've seen some thoroughbreds. He's fit for a queen to ride, only he wouldn't be safe. Well done! I can see he is going to be another of your triumphs!" And he went off looking quietly pleased.

Cartright was pleased too and he patted me and made much of me. I began to wish that I could do something in return for all they had done for me, for I had been given back something I had nearly lost for ever. The redemption begun by the Red Dane was in a fair way to being carried through happily. I *did* get the chance to show that there was something in me as well as kicks and bites, but I must tell of that later.

The day of the polo-match arrived and I felt so much at home now that I too began to get excited about the outcome and to take pride in our team. Scotsman was a bit jumpy as the hour drew near, but he did not show temper and he did not snap at anyone.

"Wouldn't help," he explained, with a sly look at me as I hung down my head and lipped at a wisp of fallen hay. I

was really disappointed that I could not go to the grounds
in the town where the match was to be held, but I watched
the team go off and I stood eagerly most of the day with my
head over my half-door, watching out for them.

Major Lyle himself always rode Scotsman, and the rest
of the team consisted of his army friends, who had trained
and played together for years. All was very quiet now and
only the lads were left to look after us. It was the first time
that Jim had been left entirely by himself to bring me my
two o'clock hay, and both he and I were as jumpy as scalded
cats.

He opened my door and came in, trying hard to brazen it
out as he had seen Cartright do, but, oh, what a difference
was here! We sidled about, I trying to keep out of his way
and he just as anxious not to get too near. All at once a deep
pain smote me that I should have become something of
which a child should be afraid. How far, far down I had
gone since the gipsy days when the children had played
about my feet without a hint of fear. And that ended my
troubles! I stretched out my neck to touch the lad's sweater
in a kiss of peace.

Plucky kid that he was, he responded with hearty joy and
put his arms about my neck as once, long ago, another boy
had put his.

"Good old Trold," he whispered. "They said if I liked
I could be your stable-lad and I *did* like and I will be!"

After that he couldn't tear himself away, but fussed about
me and Flopsy, cleaned out and made up my bed, and then,
at last, regretfully, left me to doze. Happy dreams coloured
my thoughts.

After the match the team came back and all the men
stayed at Windywold for dinner. But, like true sportsmen,
they thought first of their mounts and came right into the
yard to have a last word with Cartright. Everyone was

cheerful and full of jokes and allusions to the great match that was just over. They were tired to death, but a jollier crowd you could not wish to meet.

The ponies were tired too and grateful for the expert care and attention they received at once. Scotsman settled himself down at last in his straw with a sigh. I was bursting with curiosity.

"Well," I asked excitedly, "was it a great victory for us again?" To hear me, I might have been at Windywold for years. Pride in our team was now as dominant in me as pride in my blue blood or my circus tricks had once been.

"It was a grand game!" Scotsman answered, almost chuckling again. "But *they* won, you know. They were a better lot than we were, this time, so they deserved it. They must have trained themselves out of their boots nearly to win, but it doesn't matter a bit."

"It does matter," I said stormily. "I hate them for winning!"

Scotsman looked amazed. "You are no polo-pony, of course, or you'd have more sense," he said, almost coldly for him, for he was a dear little thing. "They were all old regimental friends, so no one cared a scrap. It was the game that was the thing! Now we're all keyed up to meet 'em and beat 'em next year. Go to sleep now. Am I tired!" And he shook himself.

I was stunned at his queer outlook and I thought over it for a long, long time that night. Here was a strange new standard with which to measure life. "The game was the thing." If it applied to polo, it might apply to all things. Do your best, and win or lose the game was worth it!

I hadn't always done my best when it happened to suit me not to; on reflection, however, I saw that it must be a code by which many men lived: Andrea and the Red Dane and Haldane and Melville too. *Well,* if *they* believed in it

it was all right. It took all the sting and the hate out of my
memories and is one of the reasons why I am so happy now.
If only today's colts would listen to the horses of yesterday
when they give advice! But we must all find out for ourselves. I did not believe my mother when she told me to do
my best, but then I knew her for so short a time. Ah, well,
it is no good sighing for what might have been!

I must now tell of the time when I really got a chance to
do something in return to please Cartright and show him
that his faith in me was justified—that there was something
worthwhile under my flashy temper.

It was the spring of the year following. By that time I
had nearly forgotten that I ever started at shadows or kicked
at rats. The family had not been at Windywold all that time,
but I had. They often went off in the winter to the south of
France, but I was very happy with my good friends, Scotsman and the ever-faithful Flopsy, who had batch after batch
of sturdy kittens and became a great name as a mouser. The
stable-lads adored her and brought her ribbons and titbits,
which she acknowledged with the same regal indifference,
blinking her inscrutable eyes at them.

In March the family returned and I heard rumours of a
move to London, to which they went every year. The
Major's grandson, a round-faced boy of eight, came to stay
with them and made great friends with Scotsman, but he
would not come anywhere near me, having, I suppose, been
told such tales of my old-time temper. It hurt me much to
see him shrink when I was led out into the yard. I was, I
knew, the finest beast in the Windywold stables, but little
Malcolm kept at a safe distance and eyed me askance.

The winter that was just over had been a very dreadful
one in that part of England. Near Christmas the skies had
darkened with grey snow-clouds that piled up from the
north-west with a mounting threat. Then down came the

cool little snowflakes, twinkling and drifting, to tickle the face and blow into the eyes, seemingly harmless. But when they had been falling for days on end the depth became dangerous, and still the snow thickened and deepened and more and more fell.

When, at last, the rains of February came to wash away the slush, floods began to spread. Down in the township of Peterly and on the flat grounds of the valley it soon became serious, for the water could not be got away fast enough. Quicker than it flowed down the river—now a lake for all its length—more melting snow came washing down the crag-sides. The flood-level rose inch by inch, creeping relentlessly up against the house walls till it lapped the sills of the lower windows; men must go in boats to get the people out.

We were luckier at Windywold, which stood outside the town on much higher ground. But we were miserable enough, for everything was boggy and soaked through, our draughty stables seemed more chill than usual, and often and often supplies could not be got through to us. But through it all I was very content; my lonely heart was warmed by kindness and the trust of these good people. I felt as if the roughest winds that ever blew could not get through my armour.

February then was wild and wet. Everything was late. The floods drowned the early flowers, so there was no cheerful gold of crocus in the cottage gardens, even where these were up the slopes and not covered by the floods. The crops of carrots and beets, stored securely against frosts, rotted away in a few days when the flood-water, about which no one had dreamed, reached them and washed open their earth-coverings.

Rickety old cottages, some of which had stood for hundreds of years, were undermined and collapsed in a cloud of rubble and brick-dust, soon quenched by the swirling water. Many, people were drowned, and almost every day the bell at St. Martin's rang dolorously across the seas that once had been barley-field and waving corn-land.

In the north part of the town nearer the station, where the ground was higher, it was still possible to get about with only a foot of water over the streets. I hated doing this, as I don't like treading on ground I can't see, but I was the only one of all of us who could be relied on not to jib or shy; none of them had seen flood-waters before, whereas I had not only seen the sea but had swum back to safety through it, so was cool and dependable.

Cartright, I knew, was overjoyed at this, for it showed how right he had been to say, as he had done over and over again, that if I were allowed time to get over my temper I would. I would have risked a lot to please him. I liked the little man who had mastered me with quiet kindness. The very sight of his bandy legs made me prance and nicker.

CHAPTER TWENTY-ONE

RESCUE

"CARTRIGHT, there's a load of stuff come through on the ten-thirty for us," the Major said one afternoon. "Put one of the horses in the light cart and fetch it, will you? I can trust you!"

"Yes, sir!" The headman touched his fingers to his forehead. "I'll take Trold."

His master, who had been turning away, paused and looked doubtfully at me where I stood with my head over the half-door, watching the quiet afternoon comings and goings. I noted even then how lowering the clouds seemed and how the March wind was beginning to moan and sing about the place, banging unlatched doors and flicking up wisps of straw and hay to whirl roof-high. The Major did not know how often already I had been down to the flood area and that I had done all the errands for Windywold for the past two weeks.

"I suppose you can trust him, Cartright? You know, with his record, if he were to start breaking things up just when you wanted to rely on him——"

Cartright smiled. "That's all right, sir. Trold and I will get the stuff!"

He harnessed me with care and I neighed to him, for I liked the work very well. We were just setting off when the rain began to fall again, heavier than ever. The Major came running out of the house as we turned down the drive, but he was a different man from the pleasant, easy-going soldier who had sauntered into the yard a while back to give Cartright his orders. His face was just like one of those images carved in hard grey stone in old churchyards and his eyes were dreadful to see. He boarded the lightly bowling cart with the skill and agility of a boy.

"Never mind the station! Make for the river below the bridge," he gasped. "And, for heaven's sake, man, drive as you never have before. I'd take the reins, but I feel you know Trold better than I do!"

"What's to do, sir?" Cartright asked anxiously as we turned out of the great gates into the boggy ruts of what had once been a good road.

Go as carefully as I could, the two men were flung about like peas in a shaken pan. All the time, the rain ploughed down.

"It's Malcolm! Word was just brought ten minutes ago. He'd gone to look at the floods—listened to the servants' chatter, I expect. He and some friends of his, old Colonel Everard's boys, tried taking a boat to see the sights. Someone saw them in trouble out on the wide part where the wrecks of those cottages are. Men are trying to find a boat still strong enough to stand the strain of going after them, but they've all had such a battering lately."

"What are you going to do, sir?" It was characteristic of Cartright that he wasted no time with the "you don't says" and silly side-chatter of excited gossips.

"I hardly know!" Major Lyle's voice was weary and broken. "But we'll get there and see. They may have got out of their pickle by the time we get there. I hope so; I trust and hope so!"

"We'll turn off down this street, if you please, sir," Cartright said.

I was already in water over my knees, but now at once it was deeper, so that I was almost washed off my balance. The shafts of the cart helped me. And this, mark you, was

not the lowest-lying part of the town. The footing was
horrible, as it had been an unpaved lane down to the river.
However, I did my very best, straining to keep going. I
made good time and I heard the two men behind me com-
ment on my sure-footedness and lack of fear at what might
have upset most animals. Then we came out into what had
been wide fields just before the river, only now it was a lake
nearly a mile across. Down the centre, winding and twist-
ing in its old channel, was the river, now a millrace of flood-
water.

Branches and wreckage, fantastically turning and bowing
with the wavelets, were carried majestically past; chips and
drowned fowls, old chairs and papers, and a hundred other
things went sliding by on the brown water, laced with foam-
patterns. On what had been the far bank stood the half-
uprooted remains of an oak, the acorn of which I had heard
Cartright tell the stable-lads many a time must have been
dropped there in King Canute's time. But storm and flood
had at last been too much for the old shell. At each impact
of driven rubbish and swirling water the old tree shook and
trembled, leaning so far over that it was already half under
the surface.

But it was not this which made the two men groan.
Clinging in the branches where their frail boat had smashed
itself were four boys, one of whom was Malcolm. They
were shouting and laughing in great feather, for they were
too young to realise how serious it all was. To them it was
a huge lark, an adventure like those about which they read
in their books.

"What to do?" Major Lyle asked, and his voice had gone
little and cold and empty, like the autumn pods rattling on
a tree-lupin. "Can we drive as far as the old river-bank?
If the horse is all you say as far as wits go he'll not slip over
the edge!"

There was a pause. "I don't see what good that would do, sir," Cartright answered calmly. "We must reach them. I have a better plan, sir, begging your pardon. Will you help me? We'll unharness Trold!"

"What are you going to do?" the Major asked sharply. "I'm afraid I haven't all your confidence in him. He looks a bit of a brute when he rolls his eyes till the whites show. I believe he's terrified."

"Terrified? *Him?*" Cartright positively snorted. "No, sir; that's one thing about a high-mettled animal, he'll go the whole length you ask, even if it breaks his heart. His spirit won't fail, never fear!" All this time he had been in water almost up to his armpits, unharnessing me, and then he and the Major led me out.

"I'm coming too!" our master said firmly.

"Begging your pardon, sir, you are not. You'd be in the way, and one more for the horse to drag, and he trusts and understands me. Truly, sir, it would be best."

"I can't bear to be left." The poor Major was wringing his hands in desperation. "He's *my* grandson."

"I know, sir, and that's partly why it must be me who goes."

Without waiting for more, Cartright scrambled on to my back and urged me forward. He had shortened the reins. "Now, my beauty," he said, "we'll show them what we can do, eh? You take over. You know where you are going!"

I braced myself and plunged forward, the roily water eeling all about me. The ground sucked at my feet and I had to go very slowly, but I knew I should be able to tell when we reached the bank, for the uncertain footing would warn me. Somehow, solid ground echoes back to us in a queer way and the feelings of safety or trembling insecurity are as distinct to us as are the newspaper headlines to a man. So I went forward boldly and as fast as I could.

The boys had seen us and set up a great shouting and laughing, calling us rescuers of shipwrecked mariners and other nonsense. On higher ground, far off on the other side, people were standing to watch.

I reached the bank and gave a scrambling leap forward into deep water. At once I struck out to swim, but I was amazed at the pull and rush of the current. There had been nothing like this in the salt sea that time I had carried Flopsy to safety eighteen months ago. But instinctively I turned to swim a little bit upstream against the drag. I saw what was coming almost before I heard the shout of warning from behind. Even the boys had at last sensed that this was not just a game but the most terrible reality. They fell silent, and four white faces stared helplessly upstream.

Coming down toward them was a mass of wreckage which had been tangling together for miles back and was a mix-up of torn-out floorboards, wrecked boats and landing-stages, pig-pens and hen-coops and all the odd bits of timbering which usually spring up along a river-bank at the bottoms of gardens leading down to it.

"We must get to them first," Cartright urged me, but his voice was not so ringingly confident as it had been. "Cheerily does it, Trold. We will show them!"

But struggle on as I might, the mass of flotsam was gaining on us. It rolled slightly as it came, borne on the swirling water, sidling first a little to the right, then swinging to the left.

I thought I had swum desperately in that effort to beat the salt-tide on the Essex coast, but I had loitered then compared with the race which I put up now to beat the coming disaster. I could hear Cartright muttering encouragement to me, but that was all he or anyone could do. And then I saw that we were not going to make it, after all.

"Heaven help them," the man almost sobbed.

There was a rending crash as the wreckage hit the old oak. The boys screamed in real terror, but they clung on in despair, for to take to that millrace of water would have been suicide indeed. The tree might hold out for awhile and stave off the tragedy long enough for us to reach them. But it was shaking so violently that the great branches waved and dipped. The boys were, of course, on the worst possible side as far as rescue went. They were on the downstream side, with all those tons of wreckage towering above and behind them. We must swim in under this menacing wall, from which whining creaks and jarring cracks were sounding.

"Hurry!" Cartright urged me, and I responded with every last ounce of strength I had. I remember looking with dilating eyes at that wreckage and noting little, absurd things which I remembered long after. But I was not afraid. A kind of steely determination to do my best gave me a warm kind of inner strength. I saw a child's doll, headless, pinned between two huge beams, and a cheery bit of red ribbon, and a tin pail squashed and flattened, its handle screwed up as if it had been limp string. But I found to my joy that here was a ridge of silted-up ground, which had once been the little headland on which the oak had stood. I was able to find footing and steady myself and Cartright noted it. I heard him shout to the boys.

"If this bank is not too steep we may not have to re-cross. We'll get out this side!"

They were climbing down towards us, hurrying too much in their terror, for they were shaking the mass badly.

"Steady now," the man warned. "Plenty of time."

That, of course, was where he was wrong and he knew it. Then the first of the lads reached us. Cartright slipped off my back and held on while assisting the other three. What a long time it seemed before Malcolm, who was last, was astride of me. The man looped his left hand in my mane.

"Now, cheerily does it. Forward, Trold!"

I could hear the faint cheering from the distant mass of people who were watching us. Even if I had not understood his meaning, I should have attempted to climb out here, so I struck out for where the banks had once been. The current was stiffer than ever, or was it because I had now more weight and responsibility in my care, or was it because even my magnificent spirit and strength were tiring?

Anyway, a feeling of bleak despair chilled me, and as I heard behind us the creaking smash as the oak finally uprooted I knew that that threatening mass was once more unleashed. Head up, nostrils gaping and eyes staring desperately, I struggled on. I heard a wail of terror from the watching crowd and so I knew that the mass was gaining on us.

Then I felt the ground below my feet and knew that we *might* make it! Yes, this was a sloping bank and the ground was not so bad as where I had first plunged in on the opposite side. This was firmer footing.

I made a supreme effort and fought my way up, to stand with the water only breast-high in the flooded fields, away from the sucking current. I was trembling so that I could barely stand and I knew that I had hurt my back. But no matter. We were out of it.

Just as we left the river the mass gained on us and passed, circling and nodding ponderously as if, after all, paying homage to the grit and courage of man and beast who had dared so much and won through.

F

CHAPTER TWENTY-TWO

WE MOVE TO LONDON

ENDLESS seemed that long limping misery across those flooded fields. The boys refused to ride and add their weight to my pain. Even though the water was very deep for them, they slipped off and set out pluckily enough. We made our way all together, up and out of the flooded valley.

How good everyone was to me! Colonel Everard sent his horse-box to get me home, and the carriage met us on the higher ground to collect Cartright and the boys. We had to go miles to the south before we could get across by a bridge. How Major Lyle got home I never knew.

How lovely it was to be back at Windywold and see all the admiring faces and hear all the nice things the grooms and boys said about me. Even Mrs. Lyle, who had been terrified of me ever since I had stood in my loose-box in her stables, brought me titbits, and patted and loved me and said I had a noble face and people should be shot who called me vicious.

The vet came and shook his head over me, but he was a good man and said that complete rest would probably effect a cure. So I was made very cosy on such an immense bed of straw that I nearly bounced on it. And, at his suggestion, some of the chilling draughts were stopped up. I bid fair to be very well off indeed.

The floods went on rising for another week and then they passed the peak and the worst was over. Gradually the waters went down and the soaked and soggy fields appeared again. Many thousands of pounds' damage had been done,

they said, in our valley alone. In many other places it had
been worse, for the floods had been all over England in the
low-lying parts. Relief funds were opened, but even with
their help there was much hardship. I used to hear the men
talking about it as they worked round the place through
those long, boring, idle days while I was resting.

But my back improved steadily. All that summer I took
it easily. Towards autumn they began giving me very light
exercise; the vet kept an eye on me and everyone petted me.
I was a great favourite and something of a hero in the township. Malcolm adored me and he begged and begged his
grandfather to let him have me, but Major Lyle shook his
head.

"Not for you, son," he said gravely. "He is a fine animal,
a magnificent animal, and I owe him and Cartright more
than I can ever repay. I can reward Cartright and I have
done, and I shall do more, but for Trold there is nothing I
can do except keep him from the chance of ever becoming
vicious again. I will never sell him, lest he fall into evil
hands. I will protect him from his own temper to the very
best of my power."

"But he wouldn't be vicious with me," Malcolm cried
in all the vainglory of his age. "I understand horses, honest
I do, Grandpa, and I would——"

"That will do," the Major said firmly, and he would hear
no more. In a way, I suppose he was right.

At their appointed time the family went to London, and
Windywold was very quiet. When the local polo-season drew
near they returned, and once more the place felt like home.
Windows stood open, carpets and hangings were beaten and
shaken. There was a chatter from the maids' quarters and
the rattling of buckets and mops once more.

Flopsy continued calmly to people the stable world with
fubsy offspring. Altogether everything seemed very ideal,

if a little aimless. It was the work I missed, and I used to envy Scotsman, who would come in with the team, played-out, their coats dark with sweat, their boots white with dust, but with the feeling of a hard day's grand work behind them.

About October of that year the vet said I was cured and that I could have work again. Did I rejoice? I could have kicked down the stables in my joy.

"Tell you what," Major Lyle said; "we'll take him up to London with us instead of old Ruby. He'll do nicely for me. I'm not a heavy man and it won't be heavy work such as he might take on here. He's so spirited, it's difficult to keep him in and prevent him doing more than he should. I'll take him out tomorrow, Cartright, and judge. On that depends what we do!"

I was excited, I can tell you. Here was my great chance at last. I found him an excellent rider and I did my very best, hoping my paces would suit him. We tried a canter and a short gallop. It was lovely to be flying along again and he laughed and patted me.

"Well done, Trold. I don't see why you shouldn't do very well for me."

So that was settled and very soon all the preparations were made. The rest of the family were away shooting somewhere in the north on a friend's estate, but the servants shut up the great house at Windywold. Cartright was left, as always, in charge of the stables and ponies, with his lads under him. A few maids stayed to keep some rooms aired in case any of the family returned unexpectedly. I didn't worry about Flopsy, because there was not one of those boys who would not have been shot rather than see harm come to her. And they all said I should be back in the spring.

When Cartright led me out for the trip to the outer world he joked and laughed. "Rising in the world, aren't you? Going to London with the Major. Who knows but you may carry the master in the Row. You will have seen a lot and done a lot by the time you come back to Windywold again."

That was where he was wrong, for I never returned. He put me in charge of John, a bright and painstaking undergroom who with Jim had had sole charge of me now for over three months. He was to ride me by easy stages to my new home.

One bright autumn day we set out. There had been just enough frost the night before to edge the fallen leaves with silver bands. The air was heady, the sky a clear light-blue. The haze from cottage-garden fires hung low in the bushes and drifted lazily. As we went along, I could not help thinking how once I should have capered and danced instead of getting on soberly with my work.

We had a beautiful stretch of country before us. We passed humble hamlets where, in the small lean-to sheds, the year's harvest of drying onions hung like golden globes. We went through quiet market-towns where all had been fuss and bustle only a few weeks back, at cattle-fairs and horse-shows. We saw the country schools newly white-washed and with their windows polished to a tremendous pitch of cleanness; out of them came a hum and buzz of learning. Then, on the third day, the townships became more frequent and reached out to one another over the green land between, until at last, after a week's journey, there was no green land any more, but slag-heaps and dark, oily rivers with slow barges towing on them, and great dumps of unwanted iron in forgotten yards. Then we came to mean streets and tumbledown houses and sheds.

I must say I was horrified and wondered how anyone could endure to live here. We met horses here who were real city workers, who had never since their foal days rolled on the buttercups or stood below shady trees flicking away the flies. Their quiet, patient faces spoke of toilsome lives

wherein they looked for few pleasures except their midday
nosebags of dinner and their long sleep at night.

There was now a lot of traffic about, but I had become
much steadier and only shied once when a train ran shrieking over a viaduct just above the road I was on. It was most
thoughtless!

Taller and blacker grew the houses, thicker and thicker
the crowds of people. I wondered how anyone ever steered
a dogcart, let alone a big carriage, among all these shouting,
milling folks. There were men on bicycles, dogs running
loose and barking, horses, vans, carts and drays. Often
we were completely halted and had to wait till a man in
blue with a bull's voice and the face of a good-tempered
sheep-dog sorted us out and got the stream moving again.
The roar of the rolling wheels seemed to get into my head
and bewilder me and I began to think we should never get
to our stables.

Now we got into a better part: street after street all full
of traffic, the sidewalks crowded with people, the shop-fronts
all a-glitter and full of fine things. We were getting to the
West End of London.

I knew that John was getting tired and I could tell he
was nervous. Then the streets got much wider and cleaner
and I caught glimpses of green parks. We turned up a
narrow, cavern-like street between the backs of big, fashionable houses, and there was a funny little square tucked away
by itself. All the buildings were stables and quarters for the
men and grooms. Over a wall was printed a name which I
had heard tell of many times back at Windywold: Park
Place Mews.

I was turned into a stall in one of the other stables—not
ours, because owing to some oversight they were still being
whitewashed. So on that first day I stood among common
London workhorses. I had never had much chance of talk-

ing to any such and the time was when I should have sneered and shied. But life is humbling. Now all I felt was a burning eagerness to discuss this great, terrifying new place with someone who was actually living and working here and who had, apparently, managed to survive the horrors. The stalls were very small and sloped badly. They were poorly lighted too, and after my life in country greens and the open air I felt boxed-in and rather uncomfortable. A fat little grey horse was just clearing up his corn, and he turned to stare as I came in. "My word!" he said, shaking his head. "Here's class! Here's one of the top-jossers. Blue blood, I *should* say. What are you doing in here?"

I explained, feeling very small and unimportant, after all. The world was so big, much, much bigger than I had ever dreamed. What did my little bit of service or love matter? I said so and the grey horse stamped indignantly. "That's a stupid, short-sighted kind of attitude," he grunted. "Look at me. Milk-horse! Most important! The people in Soper Street and Bray Street and all round there just couldn't do without me. I'm round with the cans before five o'clock, I can tell you. The folks in the houses over by the Park don't know me, have never even heard of me, but that's not going to worry *me*! You can't influence the world, but you can leave your memory in your own stables!"

"What's your name?" I asked humbly.

"Beauty," the little fellow said, and never saw the queerness of it all, for he had an unhappily shaped head, with a lumpy nose, docked mane and thick legs. But he was content with it all and I was envious of him. We chatted away and he admired my good looks and listened to my stories of the country outside London, which he had never seen. And he told me of London.

"And don't let the noise get you down," he advised. "Noise can't hurt you if you don't let it. Just shut yourself away from it in your own mind and get on with the day's work!"

I felt cheered and comforted, and when, next day, they came to put me in our stables I thanked Beauty heartily.

"That's all right, chum," he said. "All the best!"

CHAPTER TWENTY-THREE

THE DARK THREAT

OUR stables were further along the Mews and there were one or two old friends from Windywold—the carriage-horses and Mrs. Lyle's riding-horse.

I waited quite eagerly for my first ride out with the Major into the busy world whose voice came to me in this little corner as a distant trembling thunder of sound. But day followed day and I stood there with nothing else to do. When they exercised me it was in the quiet backyard streets round the Mews. Can you wonder that I got bored? It would not have been so bad if my stall had had light enough in it to see about, but even at high noon it was gloomy.

Hour after leaden-footed hour, the day passed by. Often I dozed, having nothing better to do, so that I was wakeful and restless at nights. When they led me out to exercise I often stumbled, for it quite hurt me to come suddenly into the blinding flash of the daylight. Had I been there very long my sight and health would have been injured, but events were hurrying on. One day the Major came to see us and inspect our quarters and I hoped he would say something about the lighting; but, no; evidently he was used to it, and took it as a matter of course. He directed for me to be saddled for him the next day.

I was so pleased at this break in my monotonous life, for I felt myself growing restive and irritable, and above all things I did not want to become bad-tempered again. That would be a poor return indeed for all the kindness they had shown me. So next morning Eastman, the Major's headman here at the Mews, took me round to the front of a fine big house overlooking the Park. I felt much happier, almost as if I were going on a holiday.

Eastman touched his cap as the Major came out in riding kit, looking every bit the soldier and gentleman he was.

"Anything to report?" he asked, patting my nose gently and as if he loved me. "I say, Eastman, this fellow will create a demand for Essex thoroughbreds when my friends see him. That was a strange history he came with from Edlund's. Wonder what was at the back of his being wild on the marshes? Well, we shall never know!"

"No, sir," the headman answered respectfully. "Some mismanagement somewhere, I expect. And talking of management, sir, John wishes to leave at the end of the week. Shall I get someone in his place, sir?"

"Why, yes, of course. I'll leave that to you, Eastman. Have you anyone in mind?" The Major had mounted me and was sitting looking down at his man, and smiling, as I knew by the tone of his voice. "You're a regular old caution, Eastman. You've already found someone to take John's place and you're trying to get round me."

"Well, perhaps I have and perhaps I haven't," Eastman hedged. "But for the time being I have heard of a man who could lend me a hand, just a temporary."

"I leave it to you," the Major repeated.

That ride was wonderful. The air was like ice, but the parks still flaunted a few very late, last flowers, and there were plenty of people about. It was a new side of London to me. We went along the Row and had some famous gallops. My master was evidently well known and stopped to chat to many friends, who admired me but kept a distance from my heels. I began to think that life here was not going to be too bad, though the thought of going back to that ill-lighted stall in the Mews was a saddening one in the midst of joyous sunshine. But back I had to go.

In due course John left, and for a day or two, until the new man came, Eastman found that he had quite plenty to do with four horses on his hands. Grooming one horse is no weakling's job if heart is put into the work, and unless the work is done properly the horse's coat will not shine nor be really clean.

So poor Eastman had to put his back into it, and he never skimped us. He was looking forward to the Wednesday afternoon when the new man was due, I can tell you.

How well I remember it all! The time was getting on for four o'clock; indeed, the clock on the wall outside had just given off four croaking notes and then jarred into silence again. It was time for my exercise, so Eastman took me out. He had not sat down all the day and his face was grey and tired.

"Thoughtless not to turn up when he had promised," he muttered. "No matter; come along, lad! We'll stretch those long legs of yours."

We went along our old familiar streets, and I, to whom these little outings were a great break, stared about eagerly, though I knew every detail by now. I recognised all the alley-cats of all the different basements, the rosy-faced cook at number nineteen who sometimes had a crust of bread for me. I think she liked Eastman, and often called to him as we swung by.

It was a foggy day. Visibility was not very good and the November sky was out of sight altogether behind the brown roof of fog, which seemed to lie so low that it stretched from rooftop to rooftop. There was a cold bite in the air which made the people on the streets hurry along rubbing their hands together or chafing their noses. But I was happy and quite content, though I was putting up with discomforts and conditions which would have driven me crazy as a colt. We all grow in patience with the sweeping years.

But it was when we got back that my little world collapsed about my ears. The new man had come and was lounging at the stable-door in a way which Cartright would not have tolerated for a moment. I had suspected that Eastman was not such a good judge of character, but his ability and kindness with horses made him respected.

"Ah, there you are," Eastman said, dismounting, while the new man sauntered forward, touching his forehead.

It was Rice Barsard himself! What unkind trick of circumstances had caused our path to cross again? He had not recognised me, for the winter gloom was dense with the coming night. But—ah, *I* knew. I knew in every fibre of me that here was my evil genius. I had imagined that all hate had died out of me, but the memory of all my wrongs came flooding back hot as a wave of burning metal to scorch me.

This was the man who had first made me kick and bite and taught me to be wicked! I could not control myself. Eastman was holding my reins loosely in one hand as he stood near my head waiting to have a word with his new stable-man. I leaped forward, pulling the leathers out of his hand. Two bounds and then I reared high above Barsard, my hoofs flashing. I knew my eyes were ringed with white, I knew my nostrils were wide and red. I gave a kind of neighing scream.

Was I going to strike him down or was I just trying to frighten him to pay him out for all that he had done to me? I shall never know, for Rice Barsard did not wait to find out. He had only one line of escape and that was into the stable through the half-open door. He went through it like a jack-rabbit shooting down his hole when the guns are in the fields.

My hoofs struck the door a great banging thud as I came down, slamming it to. Then round I swung as sharply as ever Scotsman did in his beloved polo-games, when a horse must often turn upon a postage-stamp, as they used to say.

I lashed out with a will, and actually splintered the crazy old crossbar so that the boards bent inwards under the impact. Again and again I kicked, completely out of control. Somehow, then, all I wanted was to reach Barsard and punish him.

Windows creaked up and I heard men shouting. By this time, Eastman, who if he were easy-going was at least plucky, had collected his scattered wits. He jumped to my head, caught the flying reins and held them short, calling out to me all the time.

"Trold, Trold! Easy, lad—easy goes!"

At first I heard only the noise of his voice. In my crazy whirl of maddened excitement, I hardly felt the weight of his hold on my mouth, but gradually it came to me that I was gaining nothing.

Grooms from the other stables came running and helped him to hold me, but so worked-up was I that twice I swung three of them off their feet. I was sweating and covered with foam from my working jaws. My back where I had strained it before was aching and I was tiring. So, at last, they quieted me and I stood shaking and trembling, hardly able to breathe properly.

"Phew!" Eastman said, and he mopped his brow with a large blue handkerchief. "Phew! Thanks, fellows! They said he had been vicious once, but I didn't believe it."

"Looks quiet enough now," one of the men said.

"No, he ain't," chimed in another. "Just look at his h'eye, sir. That's the h'eye of a kicker or I'm not a Cockney. What set 'im h'off, guv'nor?"

"Nothing that I know of," said Eastman, and his voice was strained and unhappy. "I never heard of a horse so vicious that it would make a dead set at someone new in the stables. I'll have a word with the new man. Can you hold him, lads?"

"Aye, he'll not rear again. He's tuckered out," the first man replied, and indeed I did feel worn as if I had suddenly lost all my energy. But I knew that one sight of that hated face and I should be as wild again.

Eastman went into the building and I heard him talking. "Sorry this happened, my man. Hope this doesn't put you off, as I am desperately short-handed and I have never known Trold act like that, though I know he came to us with rather a bad character!"

"Trold?" I heard Barsard say, and at the very sound of his voice I laid back my ears. "Trold? Hmmmmm!"

"Do you know anything of him?" Eastman asked suspiciously. "Have you ever met him before?"

"Certainly not," Barsard lied. "But don't you worry. Perhaps I had better attend more to the others at first till he cools off. No doubt you will want to do him yourself, sir, as you said he was the master's favourite."

"Yes, I suppose we had better try that arrangement," Eastman said doubtfully. "You can do Placemate and Sarah, the carriage-horses."

They moved off to the other end of the building, still talking, and I heard no more for the moment. Then the headman came for me, led me into my stall, and worked over me till he had me dry and comfortable, well rugged-up and calmer. But every time I heard the chink of a bucket or swish of a hay-wisp from the stalls of the carriage-horses where I knew that Barsard was working back went my ears. Eastman watched me closely, a worried look on his face, as if he did not quite understand me. But he did not fear me even now, and that helped me so much. I did not feel altogether friendless in the great cold world as long as he rubbed me down and brought me my corn and "chop". I don't think he was altogether so taken with Barsard now. The man had not improved since I had seen him last. But he did manage to begin work earlier than he had used to, though he still skimped matters where he could without being detected. He was there at six o'clock next morning. I think he wanted to make a good impression. Perhaps he had not found it too easy to get situations and wanted to hold on to this one. But early as he was, Eastman was there before him and was at work when he came.

"Good morning, sir," Barsard cried, touching his cap.

Eastman grunted a greeting in reply and watched me, for I felt myself to be almost snarling like a dog, my teeth bared by my lips.

"Hold still, Trold," Eastman exclaimed sharply. "Are you sure, my man, that you've never met this horse before? It almost seems as if he had a grudge. Unintentionally, of course, you may have hurt him sometime, and a horse is like an elephant. He remembers!"

"Oh, no, sir, indeed no, sir!" Barsard assured him glibly. "I expect he's just a vicious brute, sir. I am surprised at our master buying him."

"You were hired to work, not to give your opinion on the management," Eastman said dryly and then fell silent. He kept me completely under his own hands, and, for a time, all seemed as if it were going better, though I still tried to kick if Barsard came farther than the end partition of Sarah's stall.

I fancy Eastman had a pretty serious talk about me to the Major, for I heard the other grooms discussing it and saying that the Master had wondered if he dared keep me—an animal who might suddenly go mad, as I had done, at sight of a total stranger. Who knew, he had said, what horrible accident might not occur? My future was very, very dark, and my heart sore and dispirited.

The gloom of winter and its cold seemed to have crept into me, and here in this great city there was no hint anywhere of the life that waited in the earth for the first call of spring. No birds ever sang in our narrow street, though the cheerful chirrups of the sparrows were better than nothing. We had no trees near us; there was not even a spear of withered grass in the grimy corners.

Then, two mornings later, Eastman was absent, and he left Barsard to give their food to the other horses. He had already seen to me himself.

Barsard worked about the place quietly enough. I had got more used to his presence, so that, if I did not hear him or his hated voice, I took no notice. I was not thinking of him just then, for Eastman was to be back in an hour. So I stood thinking and dreaming over past things and days of long ago, as horses will. Then, suddenly, I felt queer, cold and nervous, as if a wild beast were on my trail. It was inherited fear from times when we horses were wild too. My ears turned cold and I began to tremble. I raised my head and peered into the shadows, and there was Barsard watching me, his face working in a curious way, as if he were muttering to himself or swearing, as perhaps he was. I snorted and tossed my head, jerking it about, wishing I were free, for I felt at a horrible disadvantage, tied up by the head.

"*You* remember me!" Barsard said, talking aloud. "Oh, yes, you remembered me that first moment you saw me in the yard. I said I'd get even with you and I will, if it's the last thing I ever do! You can't bite me now and I know you hate to have me staring at you. I don't care. I just don't care what you feel like! It's no good stamping and pawing like that. You can't get away. You were the cause of me losing my place—you with your nasty temper. They tried to pretend it was rats worrying you, but it was just beastly temper. Rats—huh!"

He left his place and came sidling along for all the world like a great rat himself. I squared about with my heels to be ready for him, but the man was very quick. Wily as an eel, he slipped into my stall. He had something in his hand—what, I did not see—it may have been his old favourite, the curry-comb, with which he used to tease me to desperation.

I have said that the stalls were narrow, and suddenly I saw my chance. I could prevent his doing any mischief—I could pin him against the partition wall with my weight. I did not mean to crush him or even hurt him; all I wanted was to stop him in whatever he intended, for in this case it was I who feared him!

So I leaned on him all at once with all my magnificent weight, holding him against the woodwork. And then I think that Barsard also knew fear, for he called out in a new voice, one in which there was a high note strangling with his breath.

"Hi, you, stand up! Here, help, help! Come and hold this demon! He's trying to kill me!" But at that time the work was finished and the Mews were very quiet. "Help, help!" Barsard screamed, and then—how, I don't know—he managed to tear himself away and flung to the door, where he ran full tilt into the Major himself. Like a good master, he was coming unexpectedly, at a time when no one thought him near, to see what truth there was in the report given by his headman.

His hard, practical glance took in much more than a heedless passer-by's. He shook the trembling groom upright and then flung him on one side. Something fell from Barsard's bleeding hand, and the Major kicked it into the straw. Then he looked at me and I feel I must have been an unholy sight indeed. I felt like a demon.

"Barsard"—the Major spoke in an icy undertone, which grated as if there really were frost-particles in it—"you can consider yourself fired without a character from this second. Get out of here!" It was Haldane all over again. "And I'm going to report this matter and have you charged with cruelty. I'll see you never get another place where you have anything to do with poor dumb brutes. I heard enough and saw enough to make me sure I'm doing right. Now get out!"

And Barsard went, nor did I ever see him again.

The Major came over to me. "Poor brute, poor fellow!" he said, but he did not come close and I could not have borne it if he had. "So he was vicious because that man made him so! A pity, a great great pity, but—it can't go on!"

I did not understand what he meant just then, but when Eastman came back the Major brought him to me and the two men stood there talking in low tones, while a little lad whom they had got in hurriedly to help with Placemate and Sarah was weeping as he shook up the straw bedding and swept out the stalls.

Weeping! Why, I wondered? There was nothing to weep about now. The evil genius had gone and I felt lighter and easier, knowing in some strange way that he would never trouble me more.

"You don't really mean that, sir?" Eastman asked dubiously. "Cartright will be very much upset, sir."

The Major sighed. "I know; I know all that. So much the better that it should happen when he is not there. When we return to Windywold without Trold, he will not feel it so much, as it will have happened some time ago!"

I pricked my ears and wondered afresh. Was I going to be sold, then, if I were not to return to Windywold? But a small, nameless dread of the unknown was growing in my mind and seemed to cloud my sight, so that the stable was darker than usual.

"It can't be helped," the Major went on. "I must not sell him; my conscience won't let me so rid myself of a horse that I dare not keep myself. And he was badly strained over that business when he saved Malcolm's life. The old trouble might break out again and make him slip and come down with a rider. I could have risked that for myself, if it had not been for this other business, but I expect he's incurably vicious and it is that man's fault. Pity the beast has to pay with his life, and not the man! But at any moment he might break out—he's unpredictable now. Pray see to it, Eastman. Take him early tomorrow. I never felt so badly about anything in my life!"

CHAPTER TWENTY-FOUR

HAPPY ENDING

THE poor Major went out, sighing deeply. I saw that Eastman's face was working desperately as he tried to prevent himself from following the stable-lad's example.

As for me, I stood there sweating and shaking. Well I understood now what they meant. It was a long while before the fit of trembling passed off. They thought I was still upset by Barsard's tormenting and they dared not come near me.

But it was not that. A great fear had gripped me and I could hardly breathe. I had seen dead horses once or twice and I knew that once the magic spark had gone no power could make them move again. There would be no more sunny gallops up at Windywold, no more evening chats with pony pals in the meadows. This was the end—here in this grim, dark city where the winter fogs hung so low.

At last Eastman ventured to come to me, rubbed my ears till they were warm, rugged me up, and hand-rubbed my poor trembling legs. Then he brought me a feed of corn and patted me and tried to soothe me, but I could not eat. So he made some gruel for me, but I only blew over it, for I had no heart for anything.

It seemed so hard to me that Barsard should have been able to undo all the gentle good that the Red Dane, and, later, Cartright, had done to me. But how was I to tell these people that I was not vicious now?

The night was very long and every peal of the church bells seemed to make me quiver as the notes went *ping-ping-ping* in the hush of distance. When the gloom lightened slightly and blackness became but grey I knew it was morn-

176

ing. I think that the news of my outburst yesterday had gone round, for I was already famous in the Mews. More than one lady and gentleman had been to see Major Lyle's black Arabian in the past few days. So, when I was led out into the yard, there were quite a number of men and boys idling there, and in all the faces was regret and a dull resentment.

It was a bleak morning, intensely cold; faces and hands were blue. The distant hum of London's traffic swelled and died and swelled again with a sound as of a giant baby sighing to itself. I had often stood and listened to the street cries and I heard them again now. One of them was new to the people about me, for I saw them turn and listen. But, ah—not new to me!

"Flowers, gipsy flowers, hand-cut from wood-shavings. Come, buy my gipsy flowers!" A young gipsy boy was roaming along the streets at the back of the fashionable houses, crying his wares. "Gipsy flowers; come buy, come buy!"

He passed the entrance to the Mews, and, seeing the people, turned in, hoping for a sale. How my heart went out to him, even though I had never seen him before! His curly black pate was uncovered, his berry-brown face alight with the joy of life. It was the only sunny thing on that dark day. He was the true gipsy stock: strong as an oak sapling and with the black eyes of his race, in which all the wisdom of the stars seemed to shine. He slung his basket forward as he advanced.

"Buy my gipsy flowers, sir," he said to Eastman.

"No, not today. Cut along now, there's a good lad."

"That's a lovely horse, sir." The boy's eyes widened as he looked at me. "If I weren't always being told I'm a dreamy good-for-nothing"—he grinned at the men as if wondering at their sober faces—"I'd say I'd seen that horse before!"

One of the errand-boys in the crowd whispered something to him and I saw a look of grief pass over his face.

"Oh no, sir, not that—not a beauty like him, sir." He turned to Eastman, who had slipped on my leading bridle. *"He's* not vicious, sir. It's true, I tell you. Look at his eyes!"

"Please clear off," Eastman said shortly, for his was a hateful task. He began to lead me out towards the street and I followed because I must, my heart dumb with misery, for on the boy's clothes I could smell the old, beautiful, familiar scents of wood fires and resin and fields and heath.

He threw his basket aside and, running after Eastman, clutched at his arm. "No, sir, stop, please stop! I've remembered now. I have seen that horse once when I visited their caravan. It's Andrea's horse, it is, it is! I'd know it among a thousand. Please, sir, please!"

Something in the throbbing eagerness in his voice arrested them all and Eastman stopped and looked down at him testily, for I feel sure he was as unhappy as any of us and wanted to get his work over. But his pause added strength to the boy's insistence.

"Please let me fetch him; he's not far away. Look at the horse, sir; he *knew* that name! Oh, do let me fetch him."

"To what end?" Eastman asked. "I had my orders, boy, from Major Lyle."

"I'll go ask him, if you'll wait. Andrea would move heaven and earth to have his old horse again and he'd take him right away among us, sir, where he couldn't and wouldn't want ever to snap again. I know!"

Eastman was a humane man, and he evidently did not see why if a gipsy wanted the horse he shouldn't have it.

"No, boy, you stay here!" He scribbled a message in his notebook, tore out the leaf, and gave it to a groom with directions to take it round to the house.

Major Lyle himself came in answer to whatever he had written, and I could not help thinking there was relief on his face. The gipsy-boy, at a nod from Eastman, had scurried away like a hare to fetch Andrea.

I could hardly believe I had heard rightly, but I raised my head and looked and looked down the street; I felt as if all my hopes and longings and sick fears were in my eyes. The Major stepped up to his headman.

"This is all very extraordinary," he said. "Please explain, Eastman, why you have ventured to overset my orders!" But there was no anger in his voice.

Eastman touched his forehead, and he explained quickly. "Knowing how you felt, sir," he finished, "and not wishing to sell Trold, I thought—maybe——"

"We will see," the Major said, half frowning. "I must be convinced that it is not some hoax. How do I know that it is not some artful trick? How do we know that this fellow, Andrea, really owned this horse once? It is too easy!"

Before Eastman could reply I had half whirled round to stand listening, for I had heard a familiar step ringing on those stones as a man ran towards us. It was a step I had listened for so many, many times. I had heard it in dreams so many, many times, dreams that wakened to silence. I could hardly control myself or believe that this was not one more dream.

"Look at that!" the Major was muttering. Eastman was breathing harshly as though he had been running. The men and boys of the little crowd were pressing round, their fear of me forgotten.

And then he came, Andrea himself. But the boy-like Andrea was gone. Here was a great strong man, a magnificent figure, broadened and toughened by the years except in the heart of him. His eyes were shining strangely, his voice rang out as he saw us.

"Stardust!" Andrea called.

I neighed to him then and tried to reach him. The bridle snatched out of Eastman's hands as I strained forward, but Andrea caught it, and, not caring who stood by, threw his arms about my neck.

"Stardust!" he called again to me. "You know me all right, old fellow. The years haven't done so badly with you! You're a fine animal." He turned almost imperiously to the Major. "Little Patsy here said that you were going to shoot this horse?"

The Major cleared his throat, for there was something almost accusing in the gipsy's challenge, and, after all, the poor man had been doing his best according to his lights. Briefly he explained the circumstances, and Andrea listened, his manner softening as he heard.

"Well, let me buy him, sir," he begged. "No question of you doing anything wrong there, or loosing a vicious horse on the community. For one thing, he isn't vicious, and I'll answer for him!"

The Major looked doubtful but hopeful. "Is he really yours, or, rather, was he?"

"Stardust, sir?" Andrea laughed, throwing back his head in fierce, happy pride. "I should say he was, sir. Why, Stardust, beauty, we can prove it. Where are our old tricks, or maybe you've forgotten. Look, we'll show them. What date is it, gentlemen?"

"The eighth," one man said wonderingly.

"Good enough," Andrea cried. He dropped my reins and stepped out in front of me. "Now then, Stardust, count up to eight," he said.

How the old atmosphere came back! I was so happy, so comforted, that even those dark streets seemed rosy-bright to me now. Proudly I arched my neck, though now no plumes nor tinsel-stars adorned it. Proudly I watched for that secret signal, and then I pawed the ringing cobbles with deliberate strokes of my hoof.

The pale light of that winter's day glowed on those astounded faces and glittered in the bulging eyes. The urchins hanging on the outskirts of the crowd gaped and pointed.

"'E's a-counting hup to eight," one little creature said, rolling terrified eyes. "A 'orse what counts! 'Ere, I'm hoff!" And off he flew as if the police were after him.

When I had done there was a little patter of hand-clapping.

"If I hadn't seen that I'd never have believed it," the Major exclaimed. "I withdraw all claim, gipsy. Take the horse. I feel he will be all right with you and I'm thankful to be free of the responsibility of ending the life of anything so beautiful, but as it was I had no choice. Cartright was right; he always said there was good in Trold! But, harkee, gipsy, it is a gift! No sale, and you must promise me never to sell him yourself!"

"I would promise that," Andrea said proudly, "but I cannot take him as a gift like that."

"Not for his sake?" the Major asked, and the two men looked at each other and nodded and smiled as if race and blood did not matter if brave hearts agreed. And they were right. "Shake on it," the Major said, and they shook.

Then, without more fuss, Andrea turned to me. "May I borrow the bridle, sir. I will send it back faithfully."

"Don't you dare do any such thing. It is yours."

The small crowd stood about the Major, and they watched us go. Andrea had thanked the bright-eyed gipsy lad who had fetched him from some nearby place where he had been selling brushes.

And so I walked out of the Mews and out of my life of worry and hardship and back into the sunshine of my first love and the joy of the old life I knew and had once despised.

We went by the humble streets, and almost at once we were in a very poor part of London, where the houses were old and black with soot and leaned together as if for companion-ship. There, on an open common, was our resting-place. We had come for miles out into the suburbs.

I saw the familiar outlines of a caravan, not the one I had known, for Andrea owned his own now and had a bonny gipsy wife and a baby son, a little cherub carved in mahogany who staggered about on sturdy legs. Smoke curled up from the smokestack and at the windows were spotless curtains defying the soot and grime. The glass panes sparkled; they were so clean. Two nice little cobby-horses were picketed nearby and were pulling happily at their hay in a calm detachment of content.

The door opened and the pretty little wife that my Andrea had chosen came down the steps carrying the baby boy, Rudy. She put him down and then came towards us, for she had recognised Andrea's step and was, no doubt, surprised as she heard a horse's hoofs.

"Oh, why, how wonderful! Had we then enough money saved to buy another one?" she cried, but at sight of me she hung back a little, gipsy though she was. "Is he good?" she whispered. "There is a sad, wild look in his eyes. Once before I saw it in the eyes of a dog who had been hunted."

Andrea kissed her, and lifted up Rudy and flung the child aloft chuckling and screaming with delight.

"So he has been hunted, hunted by life," he said. "But he is happy now and we will make up to him for everything. You've heard me tell tales round the camp-fire of Stardust. Well, this is he; life had made him learn to kick and bite in his unhappiness and they were going to shoot him, but I asked for his life and—he is ours!"

She shrank a little. "A kicker? We daren't have such a horse round the camp with Rudy!" Pity starred her eyes

with tears for me, but her fears for her son were stronger.
"Oh, don't keep him, Andrea, don't!"

He laughed gaily at her fears. "Don't doubt your man,"
he chided gently. "I say it is all right. Is the meal ready?
I will get something for Stardust while you put out the plates
and cups and in the meantime we must leave Rudy to make
friends."

"Andrea!" It was a cry of stormy protest. "I won't do
it; I can't. Rudy is mine!"

"Rudy is mine, too," Andrea answered patiently. He
picketed me as he talked. "I tell you I know this horse.
Trust him and he will never betray you. Go indoors, my
woman, and make our meal. Rudy, son, come here. See,
here is a tired, lonely old horse. People have been unkind
to him and he is feeling so sad. Won't you love him a little?"

"Yes, yes, Dada!" the cherub chuckled, and clapped its
fat little hands. The wife went weeping up the stairs and
paused at the top, her gay apron to her eyes. But she trusted
her Andrea as much as I did.

He went at once to get me food, and Rudy toddled towards
me. Something inside me seemed to break at that sight and I
felt warm and joyous once again, as I had done in the old days.
The baby came right up to me and I stretched down to it and
blew gently at its little hands and it screamed with delight
and beat upon my forelegs and held up its face and danced.

"Big hoss, big hoss, hoss all Rudy's," the child announced.

That was the last turning-point in my eventful life. Truth-
fully I can say that I never kicked or bit again, but put all
sad things behind me for all time. I was wanted, loved and
trusted again and that was all that I cared about.

There is not a great deal more to say. The spring came
again and we went on the road. Andrea had soon discovered
that I had been strained and took care never to overtax my
strength.

Oh, the joy of the open road again! I hoarded every happy minute with jealous care. I found again all the old thrills: the twinkling song of the wild birds, the dust of green as it came in shifting shades on the hedgerows, and the sweet wild violets and poppies and corncockles.

London city was soon behind us, a low purple smudge on the horizon, and the world of country lanes and peaceful fields in front.

For fifteen years we travelled together, until I was twenty-three years old and beginning to fail a bit. Andrea said I had earned my rest and he meant that I should have it. So he took us into Suffolk, to Silas Weatherbeam's estate, where was kept a happy place for old horses, dogs and cats, as I told you earlier. I had watched the contented creatures living under man's protection and on his bounty as a reward for their services.

I am there now and I am well content. Andrea sees to it that his way lies often past its hospitable gates, and always he comes to see me and to bring me something. We stand together, his arm over my back while he talks to me.

They are so good to me here. I wish there were hundreds and hundreds more of these parks for us old servants who have done our best. Perhaps, in another age, there may be!

I feel in philosophic mood and I would say to all colts— take a lesson from me. Do your best, hope for the best, and love the best things there are in life: the fresh air and sunshine and the trust of a good man.

The daisies in the fields bloom for us all, and the sky is blue above the clouds all the time, for when they roll by it smiles through to us again. And fresh air and sunshine and bird-song are the same all the world over for those who see and hear in their hearts.